SELECTED STORIES

by

STEPHEN VINCENT BENÉT

British Library Cataloguing-in-Publication Data
A catalogue record for this book is available from the
British Library

Stephen Vincent Benét

Stephen Vincent Benét was born on 22nd July 1898 in Bethlehem, Pennsylvania, United States.

Benét was sent to the Hitchcock Military Academy at the age of ten and then continued his education at The Albany Academy in New York. He also attended Yale University where he received his M.A. in English.

Benét was an accomplished writer at an early age, having had his first book published at 17 and submitting his third volume of poetry in lieu of a thesis for his degree. During his time at Yale, he was an influential figure at the 'Yale Lit' literary magazine, and a fellow member of the Elizabethan Club. Benét was also a part-time contributor for the early Time Magazine.

Benét's involvement with the University literary scene led to a decade-long judgeship of the Yale Series of Younger Poets Competition. He is also responsible for publishing the first volumes of work by authors such as James Agee, Muriel Rukeyser, Jeremy Ingalls, and Margaret Walker. In 1931, he was elected as a fellow of the American Academy of Arts ad Sciences.

Benét's best known works are the book-length narrative poem *American Civil War, John Brown's Body* (1928), for which he won a Pulitzer Prize in 1929, and two short stories, *The Devil and Daniel Webster* (1936) and *By the Waters of Babylon* (1937). Benét won a second Pulitzer Prize posthumously for his unfinished poem *Western Star* in 1944.

Stephen Vincent Benét died of a heart attack in New York City, on 13th March, 1943, and is buried in Evergreen Cemetery, Stonington, Conneticut.

CONTENTS

A 1

THE NORTH AND THE WEST and the south are good hunting ground, but it is forbidden to go east. It is forbidden to go to any of the Dead Places except to search for metal and then he who touches the metal must be a priest or the son of a priest. Afterwards, both the man and the metal must be purified. These are the rules and the laws ; they are well made. It is forbidden to cross the great river and look upon the place that was the Place of the Gods —this is most strictly forbidden. We do not even say its name though we know its name. It is there that spirits live, and demons—it is there that there are the ashes of the Great Burning. These things are forbidden—they have been forbidden since the beginning of time.

My father is a priest; I am the son of a priest. I have been in the Dead Places near us, with my father—at first, I was afraid. When my father went into the house to search for the metal, I stood by the door and my heart felt small and weak. It was a dead man's house, a spirit house. It did not have the smell of man, though there were old bones in a corner. But it is not fitting that a priest's son should show fear. I looked at the bones in the shadow and kept my voice still.

Then my father came out with the metal—a good, strong piece. He looked at me with both eyes but I had not run away. He gave me the metal to hold—I took it and did not die. So he knew that I was truly his son and would be a priest in my time. That was when I was very young— nevertheless, my brothers would not have done it, though they are good hunters. After that, they gave me the good piece of meat and the warm corner by the fire. My father watched over me—he was glad that I should be a priest. But when I boasted or wept without a reason, he punished me more strictly than my brothers. That was right.

After a time, I myself was allowed to go into the dead houses and search for metal. So I learned the ways of those houses—and if I saw bones, I was no longer afraid. The

7

bones are light and old—sometimes they will fall into dust if you touch them. But that is a great sin.

I was taught the chants and the spells—I was taught how to stop the running of blood from a wound and many secrets. A priest must know many secrets—that was what my father said. If the hunters think we know all things by chants and spells, they may believe so—it does not hurt them. I was taught how to read in the old books and how to make the old writings—that was hard and took a long time. My knowledge made me happy—it was like a fire in my heart. Most of all, I liked to hear of the Old Days and the stories of the gods. I asked myself many questions that I could not answer, but it was good to ask them. At night, I would lie awake and listen to the wind—it seemed to me that it was the voice of the gods as they flew through the air.

We are not ignorant like the Forest People—our women spin wool on the wheel, our priests wear a white robe. We do not eat grubs from the tree, we have not forgotten the old writings, although they are hard to understand. Nevertheless, my knowledge and my lack of knowledge burned in me —I wished to know more. When I was a man at last, I came to my father and said: "It is time for me to go on my journey. Give me your leave."

He looked at me for a long time, stroking his beard, then he said at last: "Yes, It is time." That night, in the house of the priesthood, I asked for and received purification. My body hurt but my spirit was a cool stone. It was my father himself who questioned me about my dreams.

He bade me look into the smoke of the fire and see—I saw and told what I saw. It was what I have always seen— a river, and, beyond it, a great Dead Place and in it the gods walking. I have always thought about that. His eyes were stern when I told him—he was no longer my father but a priest. He said: "This is a strong dream."

"It is mine," I said, while the smoke waved and my head felt light. They were singing the Star song in the outer chamber and it was like the buzzing of bees in my head.

He asked me how the gods were dressed, and I told him how they were dressed. We know how they were dressed from the book, but I saw them as if they were before me. When I had finished, he threw the sticks three times and studied them as they fell.

"This is a very strong dream," he said. "It may eat you up."

"I am not afraid," I said, and looked at him with both eyes. My voice sounded thin in my ears, but that was because of the smoke.

He touched me on the breast and the forehead. He gave me the bow and the three arrows.

"Take them" he said, "it is forbidden to travel east. It is forbidden to cross the river. It is forbidden to go to the Place of the Gods. All these things are forbidden."

"All these things are forbidden," I said, but it was my voice that spoke and not my spirit. He looked at me again.

"My son," he said. "Once I had young dreams. If your dreams do not eat you up, you may be a great priest. If they eat you, you are still my son. Now go on your journey."

I went fasting, as is the law. My body hurt but not my heart. When the dawn came, I was out of sight of the village. I prayed and purified myself, waiting for a sign. The sign was an eagle. It flew east.

Sometimes signs are sent by bad spirits. I waited again on the flat rock, fasting, taking no food. I was very still—I could feel the sky above me and the earth beneath. I waited till the sun was beginning to sink. Then three deer passed in the valley, going east—they did not wind me or see me. There was a white fawn with them—a very great sign.

I followed them, at a distance, waiting for what would happen. My heart was troubled about going east, yet I knew that I must go. My head hummed with my fasting—I did not even see the panther spring upon the white fawn. But, before I knew it, the bow was in my hand. I shouted and the panther lifted his head from the fawn. It is not easy to kill a panther with one arrow but the arrow went through his eye and into his brain. He died as he tried to spring—he rolled over, tearing at the ground. Then I knew I was meant to go east—I knew that was my journey. When the night came, I made my fire and roasted meat.

It is eight suns journey to the east, and a man passes by

9

many Dead Places. The Forest People are afraid of them but I am not. Once I made my fire on the edge of a Dead Place at night and, next morning, in the dead house, I found a good knife, little rusted. That was small to what came afterward but it made my heart feel big. Always when I looked for game, it was in front of my arrow, and twice I passed hunting parties of the Forest People without their knowing. So I knew my magic was strong and my journey clean, in spite of the law.

Toward the setting of the eighth sun, I came to the banks of the great river. It was half a day's journey after I had left the god-road—we do not use the god-roads now for they are falling apart into great blocks of stone, and the forest is safer going. A long way off, I had seen the water through trees, but the trees were thick. At last, I came out upon an open place at the top of a cliff. There was the great river below, like a giant in the sun. It is very long, very wide. It could eat all the streams we know and still be thirsty. Its name is Ou-dis-sun, the Sacred, the Long. No man of my tribe had seen it, not even my father, the priest. It was magic and I prayed.

Then I raised my eyes and looked south. It was there, the Place of the Gods.

How can I tell what it was like—you do not know. It was there, in the red light, and they were too big, to be houses. It was there with the red light upon it, mighty and ruined. I knew that in another moment the gods would see me. I covered my eyes with my hands and crept back into the forest.

Surely, that was enough to do, and live. Surely it was enough to spend the night upon the cliff. The Forest People themselves do not come near. Yet, all through the night, I knew that I should have to cross the river and walk in the places of the gods, although the gods ate me up. My magic did not help me at all and yet there was a fire in my bowels, a fire in my mind. When the sun rose, I thought: "My journey has been clean. Now I will go home from my journey." But, even as I thought so, I knew I could not. If I went to the place of the gods, I would undoubtedly die, but, if I did not go, I could never be at peace with my spirit again. It is better to lose one's life than one's spirit, if one is a priest and the son of a priest.

Nevertheless, as I made the raft, the tears ran out of my eyes. The Forest People could have killed me without fight, if they had come upon me then, but they did not come. When the raft was made, I said the sayings for the dead and painted myself for death. My heart was cold as a frog and my knees like water, but the burning in my mind would not let me have peace. As I pushed the raft from the shore, I began my death song—I had the right. It was a fine song.

"I am John, son of John," I sang. "My people are the
    Hill People. They are the men.
I go into the Dead Places but I am not slain.
I take the metal from the Dead Places but I am not
    blasted.
I travel upon the god-roads and am not afraid.
    E-yah! I have killed the panther, I have killed the
    fawn!
E-yah! I have come to the great river. No man has come
    there before.
It is forbidden to go east, but I have gone, forbidden
    to go on the great river, but I am there.
Open your hearts, you spirits, and hear my song.
Now I go to the place of the gods, I shall not return.
My body is painted for death and my limbs weak, but
    my heart is big as I go to the place of the gods!"

All the same, when I came to the Place of the Gods, I was afraid, afraid. The current of the great river is very strong—it gripped my raft with its hands. That was magic, for the river itself is wide and calm. I could feel evil spirits about me, in the bright morning; I could feel their breath on my neck as I was swept down the stream. Never have I been so much alone—I tried to think of my knowledge, but it was a squirrel's heap of winter nuts. There was no strength in my knowledge any more and I felt small and naked as a new-hatched bird—alone upon the great river, the servant of the gods.

11

Yet, after a while, my eyes were opened and I saw. I saw both banks of the river—I saw that once there had been god-roads across it, though now they were broken and fallen like broken vines. Very great they were, and wonderful and broken—broken in the time of the Great Burning when the fire fell out of the sky. And always the current took me nearer to the place of the Gods, and the huge ruins rose before my eyes.

I do not know the customs of rivers—we are the People of the Hills. I tried to guide my raft with the pole, but it spun around. I thought the river meant to take me past the Place of the Gods and out into the Bitter Water of the legends. I grew angry then—my heart felt strong. I said aloud: "I am a priest and the son of a priest!" The gods heard me—they showed me how to paddle with the pole on one side of the raft. The current changed itself—I drew near to the Place of the Gods.

When I was very near, my raft struck and turned over. I can swim in our lakes—I swam to the shore. There was a great spike of rusted metal sticking out into the river—I hauled myself up upon it and sat there, panting. I had saved my bow and two arrows and the knife I found in the Dead Place, but that was all. My raft went whirling downstream toward the Bitter Water. I looked after it, and thought if it had trod me under, at least I would be safely dead. Nevertheless, when I had dried my bow-string and re-strung it, I walked forward to the Place of the Gods.

It felt like ground underfoot; it did not burn me. It is not true what some of the tales say, that the ground there burns for ever, for I have been there. Here and there were the marks and stains of the Great Burning, on the ruins, that is true. But they were old marks and old stains. It is not true either, what some of our priests say, that it is an island covered with fogs and enchantments. It is not. It is a great Dead Place—greater than any Dead Place we know. Everywhere in it there are god-roads, though most are cracked and broken. Everywhere there are the ruins of the high towers of the gods.

How shall I tell what I saw? I went carefully, my strung bow in my hand, my skin ready for danger. There should have been the wailings of spirits and the shrieks of demons, but there were not. It was very silent and sunny where I had landed—the wind and the rain and the birds that drop seeds had done their work—the grass grew in the cracks of the broken stone. It is a fair island—no wonder the gods built there. If I had come there, a god, I also would have built.

How shall I tell what I saw? The towers are not all broken —here and there one still stands, like a great tree in a forest, and the birds nest high. But the towers themselves look blind, for the gods are gone. I saw a fish-hawk, catching fish in the river. I saw a little dance of white butterflies over a great heap of broken stones and columns. I went there and looked about me—there was a carved stone with cut-letters, broken in half. I can read letters but I could not understand these. They said UBTREAS. There was also the shattered image of a man or a god. It had been made of white stone and he wore his hair tied back like a woman's. His name was ASHING, as I read on the cracked half of a stone. I thought it wise to pray to ASHING, though I do not know that god.

How shall I tell what I saw? There was no smell of man left, on stone or metal. Nor were there many trees in that wilderness of stone. There are many pigeons, nesting and dropping in the towers—the gods must have loved them, or, perhaps, they used them for sacrifices. There are wild cats that roam the god-roads, green-eyed, unafraid of man. At night they wail like demons, but they are not demons. The wild dogs are more dangerous, for they hunt in a pack, but them I did not meet till later. Everywhere there are the carved stones, carved with magical numbers or words.

I went North—I did not try to hide myself. When a god or a demon saw me, then I would die, but meanwhile I was no longer afraid. My hunger for knowledge burned in me— there was so much that I could not understand. After awhile, I knew that my belly was hungry. I could have hunted for my meat, but I did not hunt. It is known that the gods did not hunt as we do—they got their food from enchanted boxes and jars. Sometimes these are still found in the Dead Places—once, when I was a child and foolish, I opened such a jar and tasted it and found the food sweet. But my father found out and punished me for it strictly, for, often, that food is death. Now, though, I had long gone past what was forbidden, and I entered the likeliest towers, looking for the food of the gods.

I found it at last in the ruins of a great temple in the mid-city. A mighty temple it must have been, for the roof was painted like the sky at night with its stars—that much I could see, though the colours were faint and dim. It went down into great caves and tunnels—perhaps they kept their slaves there. But when I started to climb down, I heard the squeaking of rats, so I did not go—rats are unclean, and there must have been many tribes of them, from the squeaking. But near there, I found food, in the heart of a ruin, behind a door that still opened. I ate only the fruits from the jars—they had a very sweet taste. There was drink, too, in bottles of glass—the drink of the gods was strong and made my head swim. After I had eaten and drunk, I slept on the top of a stone, my bow at my side.

When I woke, the sun was low. Looking down from where I lay, I saw a dog sitting on his haunches. His tongue was hanging out of his mouth; he looked as if he were laughing. He was a big dog, with a grey-brown coat, as big as a wolf. I sprang up and shouted at him but he did not move—he just sat there as if he were laughing. I did not like that. When I reached for a stone to throw, he moved swiftly out of the way of the stone. He was not afraid of me; he looked at me as if I were meat. No doubt I could have killed him with an arrow, but I did not know if there were others. Moreover, night was falling.

I looked about me—not far away there was a great, broken god-road, leading North. The towers were high enough, but not so high and while many of the dead-houses were wrecked, there were some that stood. I went toward this god-road, keeping to the heights of the ruins, while the dog followed. When I had reached the god-road, I saw that there were others behind him. If I had slept later, they would have come upon me asleep and torn out my throat. As it was, they were sure enough of me; they did not hurry. When I went into the dead-house, they kept watch at the entrance—doubtless they thought they would have a fine hunt. But a dog cannot open a door and I knew, from the books, that the gods did not like to live on the ground but on high.

I had just found a door I could open when the dogs decided to rush. Ha! They were surprised when I shut the door in their faces—it was a good door, of strong metal. I could hear their foolish baying beyond it, but I did not stop to answer them. I was in darkness—I found stairs and climbed. There were many stairs, turning around till my head was dizzy. At the top was another door—I found the knob and opened it. I was in a long small chamber—on one side of it was a bronze door that could not be opened, for it had no handle. Perhaps there was a magic word to open it, but I did not have the word. I turned to the door in the opposite side of the wall. The lock of it was broken and I opened it and went in.

Within, there was a place of great riches. The god who lived there must have been a powerful god. The first room was a small ante-room—I waited there for some time, telling the spirits of the place that I came in peace and not as a robber. When it seemed to me that they had had time to hear me, I went on. Ah, what riches! Few, even, of the windows had been broken—it was all as it had been. The great windows that looked over the city had not been broken at all, though they were dusty and streaked with many years. There were coverings on the floors, the colours not greatly faded, and chairs were soft and deep. There were pictures upon the walls, very strange, very wonderful—I remember one of a bunch of flowers in a jar—if you came close to it, you could see nothing but bits of colour, but if you stood away from it, the flowers might have been picked yesterday. It made my heart feel strange to look at this picture—and to look at the figure of a bird, in some hard clay, on a table and see it so like our birds. Everywhere there were books and writings, many in tongues that I could not read. The god who lived there must have been a wise god and full of knowledge. I felt I had right there, as I sought knowledge also.

Nevertheless, it was strange. There was a washing-place

15

but no water—perhaps the gods washed in air. There was a cooking-place but no wood, and though there was a machine to cook food, there was no place to put fire in it. Nor were there candles or lamps—there were things that looked like lamps, but they had neither oil nor wick. All these things were magic, but I touched them and lived— the magic had gone out of them. Let me tell one thing to show. In the washing-place, a thing said "Hot", but it was not hot to the touch—another thing said "Cold", but it was not cold. This must have been a strong magic, but the magic was gone. I do not understand—they had ways—I wish that I knew.

It was close and dry and dusty in their house of the gods. I have said the magic was gone, but that is not true—it had gone from the magic things, but it had not gone from the place. I felt the spirits about me, weighing upon me. Nor had I ever slept in a Dead Place before—and yet, to-night, I must sleep there. When I thought of it, my tongue felt dry in my throat, in spite of my wish for knowledge. Almost I would have gone down again and faced the dogs, but I did not.

I had not gone through all the rooms when the darkness fell. When it fell, I went back to the big room looking over the city and made fire. There was a place to make fire and a box with wood in it, though I do not think they cooked there. I wrapped myself in a floor-covering and slept in front of the fire—I was very tired.

Now I tell what is very strong magic. I woke in the midst of the night. When I woke, the fire had gone out and I was cold. It seemed to me that all around me there were whisperings and voices. I closed my eyes to shut them out. Some will say that I slept again, but I do not think that I slept. I could feel the spirits drawing my spirit out of my body as a fish is drawn on a line.

Why should I lie about it? I am a priest and the son of a priest. If there are spirits, as they say, in the small Dead Places near us, what spirits must there not be in that great Place of the Gods? And would not they wish to speak? After such long years? I know that I felt myself drawn as a fish is drawn on a line. I had stepped out of my body—I

16

could see my body asleep in front of the cold fire, but it was not I. I was drawn to look out upon the city of the gods.

It should have been dark, for it was night, but it was not dark. Everywhere there were lights—lines of light—circles and blurs of light—ten thousand torches would not have been the same. The sky itself was alight—you could barely see the stars for the glow in the sky. I thought to myself: "This is strong magic," and trembled. There was a roaring in my ears like the rushing of rivers. Then my eyes grew used to the light and my ears to the sound. I knew that I was seeing the city as it had been when the gods were alive.

That was a sight indeed—yes, that was a sight: I could not have seen it in the body—my body would have died. Everywhere went the gods, on foot and in chariots—there were gods beyond number and counting and their chariots blocked the streets. They had turned night to day for their pleasure—they did not sleep with the sun. The noise of their coming and going was the noise of many waters. It was magic what they could do—it was magic what they did.

I looked out of another window—the great vines of their bridges were mended and the god-roads went East and West. Restless, restless, were the gods and always in motion! They burrowed tunnels under rivers—they flew in the air. With unbelievable tools they did giant works—no part of the earth was safe from them, for, if they wished for a thing, they summoned it from the other side of the world. And always, as they laboured and rested, as they feasted and made love, there was a drum in their ears—the pulse of the giant city, beating and beating like a man's heart.

Were they happy? What is happiness to the gods? They were great, they were mighty, they were wonderful and terrible. As I looked upon them and their magic, I felt like a child—but a little more, it seemed to me, and they would lay their hands upon the stars. I saw them with wisdom beyond wisdom and knowledge beyond knowledge. And yet not all they did was well done—even I could see that— and yet their wisdom could not but grow until all was peace.

Then I saw their fate come upon them and that was terrible past speech. It came upon them as they walked the streets of their city. I have been in the fights with the

Forest People—I have seen men die. But this was not like
that. When gods war with gods, they use weapons we do
not know. It was fire falling out of the sky and a mist that
poisoned. It was the time of the Great Burning and the
Destruction. They ran about like ants in the streets of their
city—poor gods, poor gods! Then the towers began to fall. A
few escaped—yes, a few. The legends tell it. But, even after
the city had become a Dead Place, for many years the poison
was still in the ground. I saw it happen, I saw the last of
them die. It was darkness over the broken city and I wept.

All this, I saw. I saw it as I have told it, though not in
the body. When I woke in the morning, I was hungry, but
I did not think first of my hunger, for my heart was per-
plexed and confused. I knew the reason for the Dead Places,
but I did not see why it had happened. It seemed to me
it should not have happened, with all the magic they had. I
went through the house looking for an answer. There was
so much in the house I could not understand—and yet
I am a priest and the son of a priest. It was like being on
the side of the great river, at night, with no light to show the
way.

Then I saw the dead god. He was sitting in his chair, by
the window, in a room I had not entered before and, for
the first moment, I thought that he was alive. Then I saw
the skin on the back of his hand—it was like dry leather. The
room was shut, hot and dry—no doubt that had kept him
as he was. At first I was afraid to approach him—then the
fear left me. He was sitting looking out over his city—he
was dressed in the clothes of the gods. His age was neither
young or old—I could not tell his age. But there was wisdom
in his face and great sadness. You could see that he would
have not run away. He had sat at his window, watching
his city die—then he himself had died. But it is better to lose
one's life than one's spirit—and you could see from the face
that his spirit had not been lost. I knew, that, if I touched
him, he would fall into dust—and yet, there was something
unconquered in the face.

That is all of my story, for then I knew he was a man—
I knew then that they had been men, neither gods nor
demons. It is a great knowledge, hard to tell and believe.

They were men—they went a dark road, but they were men. I had no fear after that—I had no fear going home, though twice I fought off the dogs and once I was hunted for two days by the Forest People. When I saw my father again, I prayed and was purified. He touched my lips and my breast; he said: "You went away a boy. You come back a man and a priest." I said: "Father, they were men! I have been in the Place of the Gods and seen it! Now slay me, if it is the law—but still I know they were men."

He looked at me out of both eyes. He said: "The law is not always the same shape—you have done what you have done. I could not have done it my time, but you come after me. Tell!"

I told and he listened. After that, I wished to tell all the people but he showed me otherwise. He said: "Truth is a hard deer to hunt. If you eat too much truth at once, you may die of the truth. It was not idly that our fathers forbade the Dead Places." He was right—it is better the truth should come little by little. I have learned that, being a priest. Perhaps, in the old days, they ate knowledge too fast.

Nevertheless, we make a beginning. It is not for the metal alone we go to the Dead Places now—there are the books and the writings. They are hard to learn. And the magic tools are broken—but we can look at them and wonder. At least, we make a beginning. And, when I am chief priest we shall go beyond the great river. We shall go to the Place of the Gods—the place newyork—not one man but a company. We shall look for the images of the gods and find the god ASHING and the others—the gods Lincoln and Biltmore and Moses. But they were men who built the city, not gods or demons. They were men. I remember the dead man's face. They were men who were here before us. We must build again.

I WAS A VERY YOUNG MAN in the publishing business at
the time—even younger, I think, than most young men
are nowadays, for this was before the war. Diana poised her
bow at the sky above a Madison Square Garden that was
actually on Madison Square—and some of the older men
in our New York office still wore the paper sleeve-protectors
and worn alpaca coats of an older day. There are young
offices and old ones: brisk, shiny, bumptious new offices
that positively buzz with expert inefficiency; and resigned,
rather wistful little offices that have come to know they will
never do well in the world. But the prevailing atmosphere
of Thrushwood, Collins, and Co. was that of substantial
tradition and solid worth. The faded carpet in the reception-
room had been trodden by any number of famous feet—
perhaps by not quite so many as I avouched to the young
men or other publishers, but still the legends were there.
Legends of Henry James and William Dean Howells and
a young man from India named Kipling who was taken for
a boy from the printer's and sent off with a flea in his ear.
New authors were always greatly impressed by our atmosphere—until they looked over their contracts and discovered that even their Australian rights had, somehow or
other, become the inalienable property of Thrushwood,
Collins, and Co. But then they had only to see Mr. Thrushwood to be convinced that their most successful works were
being published from a rigid sense of duty at a distinct
financial loss.

I had the desk that was farthest away from both radiators
and window, in the front office, so I broiled in summer and
froze in winter and was perfectly happy. I was in New York,
I was part of the making of books, I saw celebrities, and
every Sunday I wrote home about it to my family. True,
some of the celebrities were not nearly so impressive in the
flesh as in the print; but that made me feel I was seeing
Real Life at last. And there was always Mr. Thrushwood,
with his thin, worn, cameo face and his white plume of hair,

to restore my faith in mankind. When he put his hand on my shoulder and said: "You're coming along nicely, Robbins," I felt an accolade. I did not discover until later that I was doing three men's work, but, if I had known it, then, I would not have cared. And when Randall Day, of Harper's, irreverently alluded to us as "The Holy Burglars," I flung the insinuation back in his teeth, with an apt quotation about Philistines. For we talked about Philistines, then.

As a matter of fact, we had an excellent list, on the whole —for, though Mr. Thrushwood, like most successful publishers, hardly ever read a book, he had a remarkable nose for the promising and the solid. On the other hand, there were names which, as an idealist, I boggled over—and the first and foremost of these was Angela Poe. I could tolerate Caspar Breed and his lean-jawed, stern-muscled cowboys with the hearts of little children. I could stomach Jeremy Jason, the homespun philosopher, whose small green ooze-leather booklets: *A Way* *arer's Creed, A Way-farer's Vow, A Wayfarer's Heart*' *one*, produced much the same sensation in me as running a torn finger nail over heavy plush. Publishers must live, and other publishers had their Breeds and their Jasons. But Angela Poe was not merely an author—she was something like breakfast-food or chewing-gum, an American institution, untidy, inescapable, and vast. I could have forgiven her—and Thrushwood, Collins—if she had sold moderately well. But long ago, the *New York Times* had ceased to say anything about her except: "Another Angela Poe . . . sure to appeal to her huge audience . . ." before its painstaking resumé of the plot. I often wondered what unhappy reviewer wrote those resumés. For he must have had to read the books, from *Wanda of the Marshes* to *Ashes of Roses*, and I did not see how that was possible for any one man.

The settings of the novels ranged from the fjords of Norway to the coasts of Tasmania, and every page betrayed that intimate knowledge of a foreign country which can only be acquired by a thorough study of the chattier sort of guide-books. But though the scene might shift, the pup-pets remained defiantly the same. Even in Tasmania, the

21

wild roses in the heroine's cheeks remained quite un-
affected by the climate and the malign but singularly un-
intelligent snares of the cynical villain in riding-clothes.
The villains almost always wore riding-clothes, as I remember it, and were usually militant atheists, though of high
social position. The heroines were *petite*, unworldly, and
given to calling the native flora pet names. And over all,
insipid, lingering, and sweet as the taste of a giant marsh-
mallow, there brooded the inimitable style of Angela Poe.
Occasionally, this style would goad some fledgling reviewer
to fury and he would write the sort of scarifying review that
only very young reviewers write. Then the girl at our reception desk would be warned and Mr. Thrushwood would
put off all other appointments for the day. For Angela Poe
read all her reviews with passion.

It was on such an occasion that I saw her for the first
time. I was passing Mr. Thrushwood's private office, when
Mr. Collins popped out of it with a worried look on his
face. A dumpy little man who haunted the business department, he left all personal contacts with authors to Mr.
Thrushwood, as a rule. But this time, Angela Poe had
descended in Mr. Thrushwood's absence and caught him
unprepared.

"Look here, Robbins," he said, with no more preface
than a drowning man, "have we got any really magnificent
reviews on the last Poe? You know the kind I mean—all
honey and butter. The *Washoe Gazette* has just called her
a purveyor of literary lollipops—and if I could get hold of
her clipping-agency, there'd be blood on the moon."

"Why," I said, "I'm afraid I——" and then I remembered. Randall Day had the pestilent habit of sending me
all the most fulsome reviews of Angela Poe that he could
find—and one had arrived only that morning, with a neat
border of hearts and flowers drawn around it.

"As a matter of fact, I have," I said, "but——"

"Thank God!" said Mr. Collins fervently and, taking me
by the hand, he fairly ran me into the room.

But at first I could see no reason for the odd, tense look
on his face—and on that of Mr. Catherwood, our art direc-
tor, who was also there. The plump, demure, little old lady

with the face of a faded pansy who sat in the big chair opposite them had nothing terrifying about her. She was Angela Poe, of course, though ten years older than her oldest publicity-pictures. And then she began to talk.

It was a sweet, tinkling voice, monotonous and constant. And as it went on, about Mr. Thrushwood and all her kind friends in Thrushwood, Collins, and then—I could not mark the transition—about how her flowers in her wee garden were also her friends, I began to realise the secret of the look on Mr. Collin's face. It was boredom, pure and simple, but boredom raised to a fine art. For when Angela Poe was angry she did not fly into a temper any more. She merely talked in her low, sweet voice—and, as she talked, she bored, relentlessly and persistently, like a drill boring into a shell.

It was no use trying to interrupt her or change the conversation—you cannot change a conversation that has no real subject to change. And yet, as she continued, and each moment seemed longer than the last until the brute flesh could hardly be restrained from breaking into a veritable whimper of tedium, I began to realise that she knew exactly what she was about. For somehow or other, we always came back to Angela Poe and the fact that she was waiting for Mr. Thrushwood. Till I began to feel, myself, that Mr. Thrushwood's absence was a grave calamity of nature and that, if he did not come soon, I, too, might burst into tears.

Fortunately, he arrived in time, and saved us, as only Mr. Thrushwood could. Fortunately or unfortunately, for he came while I was showing her the review that Day had sent me. It mollified her greatly, though she said, in a serious voice, that of course she never read reviews. They broke the wings of the butterfly. I didn't know what she meant by that, but I must have made some appropriate response. For Mr. Thrushwood, with one of his Napoleonic gestures, informed me at five o'clock that afternoon that henceforth my salary was raised ten dollars a month.

"And, by the way, Robbins," he said, "I don't want to put too much on you—but Miss Poe liked your looks to-day. Well, Miss Poe is just beginning a new novel—I think this one is to be about Iceland, or possibly Finland—not that it matters greatly——" and he gave me a smile of complicity. "But, as you know, we always get her reference books for her and send them out every week-end—and she will have them brought by some member of the staff. It's on the west shore of the Hudson—and I'm afraid she calls her house 'The Eyrie,' " he went on, with a chuckle, "but she's really a very sensible little woman—quite a head for business, yes, indeed, quite a head," and his face held unwilling respect. "So, if you wouldn't mind? Then that's all settled. How jolly of you, Robbins!" he said, with his boyish laugh.

I had meant to tell him I would do nothing of the sort, but, while you were with him you were under his spell. Nevertheless, it was with internal revolt that I got on the ferry that week-end, with my bag of books in my hand. And then, when I got to "The Eyrie," I met a nice old lady who reminded me of my aunts. She put me at ease at once, she fed me enormously, she fussed over me with just the right amount of fussiness. The tea was solid and bountiful—I was sent to the station in a carriage and pair. To my despair, in the train going back, I discovered that I had enjoyed myself. And through my mind still ran the small, tinkling monotonous voice of Angela Poe—saying nothing, and yet, remembered. I tried very hard to place her; she was like any dozen ladies I knew in Central City, ladies with little gold watches pinned over their bosoms, who fussily but efficiently presided over strawberry festivals and sales at the Woman's Exchange. And she was not—there was something else about her, some quality I could not place. It had made her Angela Poe—and yet, what was it? Her servants, I had noticed, were perfectly trained and civil and the dog got up from the hearth-rug when she told it to get up. And yet, instinctively, you gave her your arm, when she came down a staircase. I could not make it out, but I knew, rather shamefacedly, that I was looking forward to returning to "The Eyrie." Young men are apt to be hungry—and the tea was superb.

And then, as I told Randall Day, "The Eyrie" alone was

worth the price of admission. It was one of those big wooden houses with wide verandas that the eighties built on the cliffs of the Hudson—houses that, somehow or other, remind you of grandiose cuckoo-clocks. There were the lawns and the shrubbery, the big, cupolaed stable and the gravelled drive; the hardwood floors and the heavily framed oil-paintings. It might all have come out of an Angela Poe novel—she had done it perfectly, down to the last gas-bracket. And through it all wandered Mr. Everard De Lacey, the man one must never address as Mr. Angela Poe.

It was my first experience with the husband of a celebrated authoress, and he still remains unique in my memory. You do not meet them now as often as you did—those men with the large, mobile mouths, the Hamlet eyes, and the skin that has known the grease-paint of a thousand small-town dressing-rooms. The new actors are another breed. Mr. De Lacey was not merely an actor, he was a Thespian—and it makes a difference. He must have been very handsome in his youth—handsome in the old barn-storming tradition of black, flashing eyes and Hyacinthine curls—and his voice still had the rich, portentous boom of Michael Strogoff, the Courier of the Czar. When he fixed me with his Hamlet eyes and quoted—it was The Bard—I felt ashamed of myself for not being a larger audience. But he was really very considerate about it, and I liked the way he treated Miss Poe.

For they were obviously and deeply attached to each other, those two ageing people, and one sensed the bond the moment one saw them together. They deferred to each other ceremoniously, with a Victorian civility that I found rather touching. And Everard was by no means the harmless, necessary husband such husbands often are. It was agreed that he was "resting" from a modern and sin-struck stage unworthy of his talents, but it was also agreed that, at any moment, he might return to the boards, amid the plaudits of welcoming multitudes. Later on I discovered that he had been "resting" for almost thirty years, or since Angela Poe first started to sell by the carload. But that made no difference to either of them.

"I could never have done what I have done without Mr. De Lacey," she would say in her sweet, tinkling voice and Everard would boom in return: "My dear, it was but given me to water and tend the rose. The flowers are all your own." Such things, if said, are oftener said than meant. But you felt that the Poes, I mean the De Laceys, meant them. Then a look would pass between them, the look of two souls who are linked by a deeper tie than the crass world knows.

I seem to be writing a little like Angela Poe myself, in describing them. But it was difficult, in that setting, not to become infected with Poe-ishness. If a beautiful girl in a simple muslin frock had met me accidentally in the garden and flitted away with flushed cheeks and a startled cry, I would have been embarrassed but not in the least surprised. And there were times when I fully expected to meet a little lame boy, his pale, courageous face radiant for once with the sunset glow, at almost any corner of the drive. But the De Laceys had no children, though they were extremely kind to the innumerable offspring of Mr. De Lacey's relatives. And that seemed to me rather a shame.

I had come to scoff, you see. But I remained, if not to pray, well, to be rather fascinated. They fed me well, they treated me with ceremonious politeness, they were sentimental, but generous as well. I had to listen a good deal to the tinkling, incessant flow of Angela Poe's words—but, as time wore on, I even became used to that. It was as Mr. Thrushwood had said; she could be extremely sensible, even pungent, when she wished. And she could take criticism, too, which surprised me. At least she could take it from Everard De Lacey. Now and then he would say, in his rich boom, as she sketched a scene or a character for us: "No, my dear, that will not do."

"But, Everard, how is Zepha to escape from the insane asylum, then?"

"That, my dear, I have to leave to your genius. But this passage will not do. I sense it. I feel it. It is not Angela Poe."

"Very well, my dear," she would say, submissively and turn to me with: "Mr. De Lacey is always right, you know." And he would say at the same moment: "Young Man, I am not always right. But such poor gifts as I possess are always at Mrs. De Lacey's service——"

"The fruits of a richly stored mind, Everard——"

"Well, my dear, perhaps some slight acquaintance with the classics of our tongue—some trifling practical experience in interpreting The Bard——"

Then each would make the other a little bob, and again I would be irresistibly reminded, not of a cuckoo-clock but of one of those wooden weather-prophets where an old woman comes out for fine weather, an old man for rain. Only, here, the old man and the old woman were coming out at the same time.

I hope I have given the impression that they gave me—that of two ageing people, a trifle quaint, more than a trifle ridiculous, but, beyond all that, essential to each other. For that is an important thing for a young man to see, now and then; it restores his faith in the cosmos, though he may not realise it at the time. The first taste of real life, for the young, has its frightening moments: one suddenly discovers that actual people, not in books, commit suicide in gas-filled bedrooms because they would rather die than live; one discovers that others really enjoy being vicious and make a success of it. Then, instinctively, one clings to the first security at hand, like a swimmer to an overturned boat. I wouldn't have thought it possible when I first met them, but one of the things I clung to was the De Laceys.

And as I became more and more drawn into the endless spider-web of the work of Angela Poe, I began to realise how much she owed to her husband. Oh, he could never have written anything—be sure of that. But he knew the well-worn paths of stock-melodrama in all their spurious vitality, he knew when a thing would "go." I know because, inevitably, I followed one book of Angela Poe's from conception to delivery. It was not any better, speaking from the point of view of letters, for his sugestions; for it was perfectly terrible. But it worked; it was Angela Poe; the sun rose over the cardboard mountains at precisely the right instant. And every one of his criticisms helped it on.

Then one day, when I came to "The Eyrie," she had a

touch of influenza and was in bed. He was obviously
worried about her, but insisted on my staying to tea because I always had. I had my own worries at the moment
and was glad for a breath of serenity. All his courtliness
came into play and he told me a couple of mild theatrical
jokes, but you could feel his eyes wandering, his ears listening for any sound from upstairs. If he had not been worried,
I wonder—but worry makes people confidential. I thought
it a good chance to congratulate him on his part in her work.
He listened abstractedly, but I could see he was pleased.

"Glad you think so, my dear fellow, glad you think so,"
he said. "Often I have said to myself: 'No! This time old
boy, let genius burn unhampered! Who are you to profane
the—um—the sacred flame?' But genius—even genius—
must have its trammels to bring it down to the level of us
workaday folk. And, as the—er—appreciative trammel,
perhaps I have played my part. I hope so," he said, quite
simply. "She means a great deal to me."

"I know that, sir," I said, but he wasn't listening.

"Yes," he said, "we mean a great deal to each other. I
hope she's taking those drops; you know, she hates drops.
Yes, indeed, my dear fellow. Our first meeting was like a
flash of lightning." He stared at me solemnly. "I wish that
Mr. Wedge, her first husband, could have understood it
better. But he was an earth-bound soul. He could not com-
prehend a marriage of true minds."

"Mrs. De Lacey was married before?" I said, and I
could not keep the shrillness of surprise from my voice.

"My dear boy," said Mr. De Lacey, looking surprised
in his turn, "I forgot that you did not know. She was Mrs.
Marvin Wedge when we first met," he said, reflectively,
"and beautiful as a just-unfolding rose."

A thousand unphrasable questions rose to my lips and
died there. For Mr. De Lacey continued.

"I used to call her the Rose of Goshen," he said.
"Goshen, Indiana, dear boy—I was—er—resting there at
the time, after my tour with Barrett. I played both grave-
diggers and Charles, the wrestler. Charles, the wrestler, is
not a large part, but one can make it tell. It was hard to
return to Goshen, after that, but there are financial neces-

sities. But as soon as I met Angela, I knew that I had been led. Wedge was—um—proprietor of our hay-and-feed store—rather older than I am; he used to chase me and call me Slats when I was a boy. But I had not known Angela before. She came from Zook Springs."

He paused and stared at me with his Hamlet eyes. I could see the whole scene so plainly—the dusty streets of the small town and the young, down-at-heels actor, back home discouraged, after his trial flight. I could see Angela Poe, forty years ago, in the simple gingham dress of one of her heroines. It must have all been so innocent and high-minded—innocent and unreal as a stage melodrama, even to the cynical figure of the burly hay-and-feed merchant. I could see him, somehow, in his shirt sleeves, roaring with laughter at the timid respectful speeches of—but the boy could not have been called Everard De Lacey, then. And yet, Romance had triumphed in Goshen. I wondered how.

"So Miss Poe was divorced—divorced Mr. Wedge, I mean," I said.

My companion looked curiously shocked. "Dear boy," he said, with dignity, "never once, in any of her books, has Angela Poe drawn a divorced woman."

"I know," I said feebly, though I didn't. "But in real life——"

"The books of Angela Poe are real life," said Mr. De Lacey, crushingly. Then he relented. "No," he said, "Mr. Wedge is not living. He passed over."

"Passed over?"

"Within a year of my return to Goshen. As a matter of fact, he was murdered," he said, with his Hamlet eyes fixed upon me so sternly that, for an instant, I had the horrific idea that I was about to listen to an incredible confession. But I was not. "By a tramp," he said at last. "In his feed store. For purposes of robbery. It was very upsetting for Angela."

I opened and shut my mouth, but no words came forth.

"Yes, really very upsetting. I was glad I could be with her," he said, naively. "Though, naturally, we were not married till later. She was married in a tailored dress, but she held a bouquet of orange-blossoms and lilies-of-the-valley. I insisted upon that," he said, with some pride.

"And the tramp?" I said, with youth's delight in horrors. "Was he——"

"Oh, he was never found," boomed Mr. De Lacey abstractedly, as a small sound came from upstairs, "but Angela bore up wonderfully. She is a wonderful woman." He rose. "If you'll just excuse me one moment, my dear fellow——"

"I must catch my train," I said. "But thank you, Mr. De Lacey. And be assured I shall respect your confidence," I said, trying to equal his manner.

He nodded seriously. "Yes, yes," he said. "Perhaps I should have said nothing—but, well, my dear boy, we have grown to know you and value you, in your visits to 'The Eyrie.' And they must not cease with this book—my dear fellow, no. Only, I would not bring up the matter in talking with Miss Poe. She does not like to dwell upon those days; they were not happy ones for her. Mr. Wedge was really——" Words failed him. "Mr. Wedge was really not a very sensitive man," he said.

I assured him of my entire understanding and took my leave. But, all the way home, certain thoughts kept revolving in my mind. I was not surprised that Providence, in the shape of a burglarious tramp, had seen fit to remove the insensitive Mr. Wedge. That was just the sort of thing that happened to Angela Poes. But why had she ever married him, in the first place, and how, having touched real life in her own person, had she been able to forget it so completely in her books? But those were the sorts of questions one could not ask.

And yet in the end I asked them, with youth's temerity. I asked them because I had come to like her—to like them both. And when you like people, you are apt to be more honest with them—that is the trouble.

We had planned to have a little celebration—the three of us—when the book was actually published. But it was not I who put the first copy in her hands. I brought out the dummy and the jacket. That particular Saturday Mr. De Lacey had made one of his rare excursions to New York. I was glad to find her alone, as a matter of fact, for I thought I had noticed a slight constraint between us since my conversation with him. At least, I was conscious that I knew a secret—and kept wondering if she knew that I knew. And I meant to tell her, in all honesty, how much the security and peace of 'The Eyrie' had meant to me through the year. I was only waiting a good opening. But, naturally, we started by talking publishing. Her comments were shrewd and I enjoyed them—though the influenza had left its mark, and she looked frailer than before. And then suddenly she startled me by asking what I really thought of her work.

Six months before, I would merely have buttered her, buttered her with a trowel, for the good of Thrushwood, Collins, and let it go at that. But now I had come to like her—and, after all, one has one's convictions. It wasn't the best butter, and she knew it. And monotonously, relentlessly, in her small, gracious voice, she kept pressing the point. That should have warned me, but it didn't. If authors were not megalomaniacs, no books would ever get written. But I forgot that first rule of publishing and floundered on.

"And yet, Mr. Robbins, I can feel that you don't really believe in me—you don't really believe in Angela Poe," she would say, gently and maddeningly, till at last with the rashness of youth I took my courage in both hands.

"It isn't that, Miss Poe," I stammered, "but if you'd only once—why don't you? It mightn't please your audience, but a woman of your experience—of your life——"

"My life?" she said, with dignity. "And what do you know of my life, young man?"

"Oh, nothing," I said, blundering from bad to worse, "but Mr. De Lacey said you both came from small towns—well, now, a *real* novel about an American small town——"

"So Everard has been telling tales—naughty boy! I must scold him," said Angela Poe brightly. But the brightness was all in the voice. I suddenly had the impression that she thought me a tedious young fool and wished me away. I began to long for Mr. De Lacey's return. But though I strained my ears I heard no echo of his rich boom from any corner of the house.

"Oh," I said, "please don't. They were *such* delightful stories. He—he told me you were married in a travelling dress."

"Dear Everard!" said Angela Poe. "He remembers everything. A dove-grey silk, with white collar and cuffs. I looked very pretty in it. And you think I might make a story of that, Mr. Robbins?"

"We have always hoped—your memoirs—the readers of Angela Poe——" I said.

She shook her head, decisively. "I shall never write my memoirs," she said. "Authors' memoirs never sell, you know—not really. The publishers think they are going to but they don't. And then, it would lift the veil. Do you know who I am, young man? Do you know that people write me from all over the country, every day? They write me asking me what to do with their lives. And I tell them," she said sitting up very straight. "I tell them. Very often they do it, too. Because I'm Angela Poe—and they know my picture and my books. So they can write as they might to Another," and she bowed her head for an instant. "And that is not bad for a woman who writes what you think trash, Mr. Robbins! But I always knew I could do it," she ended, unexpectedly. "I always knew I could do it. But things were put in my way."

I could not leave, for it was not my train-time yet, but I began to feel more and more uncomfortable. There was something odd in the sweet, tinkling voice—the note of a fanatic egoism almost religious in its sincerity. I was used to the egoism of authors, but this was in another key.

She passed a handkerchief across her lips for a moment. "Dear, dear, I forget so many things since my illness," she said. "What were we talking about? Oh, yes, you were suggesting an idea to me—a story about an American small town. Do you know them, Mr. Robbins?"

She asked the question so suddenly and fiercely that I almost said no instead of yes. Then she relaxed.

"But of course," she said, a trifle primly, "you do know them. You know how cramped one's cultural opportunities are. And how one is mocked, perhaps, for striving after them? Or perhaps you do not know that?"

It was a rhetorical question, obviously. So I nodded, hoping against hope for the sound of Mr. De Lacey's footfall in the hall.

"Even so," she said sweetly, "you are not a member of the female sex. And they are more easily wounded than gentlemen think. Even Everard has wounded me now and then—oh, not intentionally and I soon forgave him," she said, with a regal gesture. "Still, he has wounded." She was evidently, talking more to herself than to me, now, but the fact did not increase my comfort.

"I could have forgiven Marvin everything else," she said, "his drinking, his unbridled passions, his coarse jests. That is woman's mission—to submit and forgive. He made jokes about my housekeeping, too. And it would have cost him only eighty dollars to publish my poems. I had the sweetest wreath of field daisies for the cover. I thought he would be a way to higher things; after all, one has so little opportunity in a small town and the feed store was quite successful, financially. But I was mistaken," and she sighed, gently. I was now past wishing for Mr. De Lacey's appearance; I only wished for my train to roar into the room and bear me away. But such things do not happen, unfortunately.

"But I never thought of divorce," the mild, tinkling voice went on. "Never. It crossed my mind, once or twice, but I firmly put it aside. I have always been glad of that. I don't think he really *cared*," she said, opening her pansy eyes widely. "But he might have hurt Everard badly—he was such a very strong man. Sometimes, in the early days of our marriage, he used to carry me around the room on one arm. It frightened me, rather, but I always submitted and forgave. It was always so dusty in the store, too. It used to make me sneeze and then he would laugh. He laughed when Everard read Shakespeare to me. I sneezed

33

that evening, as I was wiping the handle of the hatchet, but no one heard me."

"As you were what?" I said, and my voice was thin and high.

"I suppose it wasn't necessary," she said thoughtfully. "It would be, now, with the fingerprints, but they were quite stupid people and we knew little of fingerprints then. But it seemed tidier—I'd let it fall on the floor and the floor was dirty. They never really swept the store. He was sitting with his back to me, reading my poems and laughing. I'd hidden the new ones, but he'd found them and broken open the drawer. The hatchet was an old one—they used to cut the wire on the feed bales with it. You know, he didn't say anything at all. He was still laughing and trying to get out of the chair. But he wasn't quick enough. I burned the money in the stove and nobody even asked me about the dress. They say salts of lemon will take out blood stains *immediately*," she murmured. "But it seemed better not to try though it was quite a nice dress."

"But weren't you ever—didn't they ever——" I babbled.

"Why, Mr. Robbins, of course," she said, with perfect placidity, "you have no *idea* of the petty malice and gossip of a small town. But I was in bed, you know, when they came to tell me—in bed with a bad cold. Any emotional strain always gives me a very bad cold—I had quite a bad one the day Everard and I were married. And everybody knew he used to sit up in the feed store till all hours, drinking and reading vile atheist books like that horrid Colonel Ingersoll's. The old cats said it was because he was afraid to go home. Afraid of me!" she said with perfect ingenuousness. "There's no limit to what people will say. Why, they even talked about Everard, though everybody knew he was driving a load of vegetables to market with his father. I thought of that before I went to the store."

"And yet," I said, "you lived in Goshen—you didn't marry Mr. De Lacey till a year later——"

"A year and a day," she corrected. "That seemed more fitting. But I went into half-mourning at the end of six months. It's rather soon, I know, but I thought I might. As long as I was to be engaged to Everard," and a faint blush coloured her cheeks. "I told him I could discuss nothing of the sort while I was still in full mourning and he appreciated my wishes—Everard has always been so considerate. At first, I thought the time would hang very heavy on my hands. But, as a matter of fact, it passed quite quickly. I was writing my first novel," she said, in a hushed voice.

I do not know yet how I got out of the house—I hope with decency. But I had left 'The Eyrie' behind and was well along on my two-mile tramp to the station before I really came to myself. It was her last words—and the picture they gave me—that sent the cold, authentic shudder down my spine. I kept wondering wildly how many successful authors were murderers or murderesses and why the police did not arrest them all. For I could see the whole story and fill in every detail. It was fatally plausible, even to Angela Poe's primness. I could even believe that if the unfortunate Mr. Wedge had paid a printer eighty dollars, he might have lived. For there are egoisms which it is not safe to mock or dam up—if you do, you are tempting the explosion of primal forces.

And then, when I had almost reached the station, I suddenly began to laugh—the healing laughter of sanity. For the whole thing was ridiculous and Angela Poe had taken an impeccable revenge. I had told her what I thought of her work—and subtly, tinklingly, convincingly, she had made me swallow the most preposterous farrago of nonsense she could think of; swallow it whole. And, in doing so, she had proved her powers as a story-teller past cavil. But once away from the monotonous spell of her voice, it was merely impossible to think of her as a murderess, and yet more impossible to think of Everard De Lacey as an accomplice. For accomplice he must have been—after the fact if not before it. Or else, she had hidden the truth from him all these years—and that was impossible, too.

For a second, I even thought of turning back to 'The Eyrie' and humbly admitting to its mistress my folly and my defeat. But my train, after all, was due in fifteen minutes, and I had a dinner engagement in New York. I would write her a letter instead—she would like a letter. I walked up and down the station platform, composing orotund phrases in my mind.

The late afternoon train from New York arrived some six minutes before my own, and I was pleased to see it disgorge the statuesque form of Everard De Lacey. He shook hands with me and boomed apologies for missing my visit. "And how did you leave Miss Poe?" he said, anxiously. "I have been away since early morning."

"Oh, she was perfectly splendid—I never saw her looking better," I said, warmed by a glow of secret laughter. "We talked for hours—she'll tell you."

"That's good—that's good, my dear fellow—you relieve me greatly," he said, while his eyes roved for the carriage that had not yet arrived. "Jenks is tardy, to-day," he said. Then he gave me a quick look. "You didn't happen to mention what you told me in our little chat when she was so ill?" he said.

"Mention it?" I said with a broad grin. "Oh, yes, indeed."

He seemed curiously relieved. "I am much indebted," he said. "Then you really do feel—and it means something coming from you—that I am of some genuine help to her? To her books, I mean—her career?"

"I do, indeed," I said, though I was now puzzled.

"Excellent," he boomed. "Excellent." He took me by the lapel with the old actor's gesture. "You see," he said, "oh, it's foolish of me, I know—and we are old now, of course. But every now and then I have the feeling that I may not really be indispensable to her. And it worries me greatly."

For the instant, as he said it, I saw fear look out of his eyes. It was not an ignoble fear, but he must have lived with it a long time.

I did not go back to 'The Eyrie'; indeed, I did not go back to Thrushwood, Collins. To do the latter without doing the former would have required explanations and I did not feel like giving them. Instead, I changed my board-ing-house, and went to work as a salesman of aluminium-ware. And, after six months of that, I went back to Central City and the place in my father's cement business that had been waiting for me. For I had come to the decision that I was not made for New York, nor the life of letters; I did not have the self-confidence of Angela Poe.

Once, during the six months, I thought I saw Mr. De Lacey on the street, but he did not see me and I fled him. And, naturally, though I tried to escape them, I saw advertisements of the last completed novel of Angela Poe. She died when I had been three months in Central City, and when I read that she was survived by her husband, the actor, Everard De Lacey, I felt as if a weight had been lifted from my breast. But he only survived her a few months. He missed her too much, I suppose, and some ties are enduring. I should like to have asked him one question, only one, and now I shall never know. He certainly played Shakespearian roles—and there must have been quite a period, after they left Goshen, when he was playing. In fact the obituary mentions Othello and Hamlet. But there is another role—and I wonder if he ever played it and what he made of it. I think you know the one I mean.

Yes, I guess, I have put on weight since you last saw me—not that you're any piker yourself, Spike. But I suppose you medicos have to keep in shape—probably do better than we do downtown. I try to play golf in the weekends, and I do a bit of sailing. But four innings of the baseball game at reunion was enough for me. I dropped out, after that, and let Art Corliss pitch.

You really should have been up there. After all, the Twentieth is quite a milestone—and the class is pretty proud of its famous man. What was it that magazine articles said: "Most brilliant young psychiatrist in the country?" I may not know psychiatry from marbles, but I showed it to Lisa, remarking that it was old Spike Garrett, and for once she was impressed. She thinks brokers are pretty dumb eggs. I wish you could stay for dinner—I'd like to show you the apartment and the twins. No, they're Lisa's and mine. Boys, if you'll believe it. Yes, the others are with Sally— young Barbara's pretty grown up, now.

Well, I can't complain. I may not be famous like you, Spike, but I manage to get along, in spite of the brain trusters, and having to keep up the place on Long Island. I wish you got East oftener—there's a pretty view from the guest house, right across the Sound—and if you wanted to write a book or anything, we'd know enough to leave you alone. Well, they started calling me a partner two years ago, so I guess that's what I am. Still fooling them, you know. But, seriously, we've got a pretty fine organisation. We run a conservative business, but we're not all stuffed shirts, in spite of what the radicals say. As a matter of fact, you ought to see what the boys ran about us in the last Bawl Street Journal. Remind me to show it to you.

But it's your work I want to hear about—remember those bull-sessions we used to have in Old Main? Old Spike Garrett, the Medical Marvel! Why, I've even read a couple of your books, you old horse thief, believe it or not! You got me pretty tangled up on all that business about the id and the ego, too. But what I say is, there must be something in it if a fellow like Spike Garrett believes it. And there is, isn't there? Oh, I know you couldn't give me an answer in five minutes. But as long as there's a system—and the medicos know what they're doing.

I'm not asking for myself, of course—remember how you used to call me the 99 per cent. normal man? Well, I guess I haven't changed. It's just that I've gotten to thinking recently, and Lisa says I go around like a bear with a sore head. Well, it isn't that. I'm just thinking. A man has to think once in a while. And then, going back to reunion brought it all up again.

What I mean is this—the thing seemed pretty clear when we were in college. Of course, that was back in '15, but I can remember the way most of us thought. You fell in love with a girl and married her and settled down and had children and that was that. I'm not being simple-minded about it—you knew people got divorced, just as you knew people died, but it didn't seem something that was likely to happen to you. Especially if you came from a small Western City, as I did. Great Scott, I can remember when I was just a kid and the Prentisses got divorced. They were pretty prominent people and it shook the whole town.

That's why I want to figure things our for my own satis-faction. Because I never expected to be any Lothario—I'm not the type. And yet Sally and I got divorced and we're both remarried, and even so, to tell you the truth, things aren't going too well. I'm not saying a word against Lisa. But that's the way things are. And it isn't as if I were the only one. You can look around anywhere and see it, and it starts you wondering.

I'm not going to bore you about myself and Sally. Good Lord, you ushered at the wedding, and she always liked you. Remember when you used to come out to the house? Well, she hasn't changed—she's still got that little smile—though, of course we're all older. Her husband's a doctor, too—that's funny, isn't it?—and they live out in Montclair. They've got a nice place there and he's very well thought of. We used to live in Meadowfield, remember?

I remember the first time I saw her after she married

McConaghey—oh, we're perfectly friendly, you know. She had on red nail-polish and her hair was different, a different bob. And she had one of those handbags with her new initials on it. It's funny, the first time, seeing your wife in clothes you don't know. Though Lisa and I have been married eight years, for that matter, and Sally and I were divorced in '28.

Of course, we have the children for part of the summer. We'll have Barbara this summer—Bud'll be in camp. It's a little difficult sometimes, but we all co-operate. You have to. And there's plenty to do on Long Island in the summer, that's one thing. But they and Lisa get along very well—Sally's brought them up nicely that way. For that matter, Doctor McConaghey's very nice when I see him. He gave me a darn good prescription for a cold and I get it filled every winter. And Jim Blake—he's Lisa's first husband—is really pretty interesting, now we've got to seeing him again. In fact, we're all awfully nice—just as nice and polite as we can be. And sometimes I get to wondering if it mightn't be a good idea if somebody started throwing fits and shooting rockets, instead. Of course I don't really mean that.

You were out for a week-end with us in Meadowfield—maybe you don't remember it—but Bud was about six months old then and Barbara was just running around. It wasn't a bad house, if you remember the house. Dutch Colonial, and the faucet in the pantry leaked. The landlord was always fixing it, but he never quite fixed it right. And you had to cut hard to the left to back into the garage. But Sally liked the Japanese cherry tree and it wasn't a bad house. We were going to build on Rose Hill Road eventually. We had the lot picked out, if we didn't have the money, and we made plans about it. Sally never could remember to put in the doors in the plan, and we laughed about that.

It wasn't anything extraordinary, just an evening. After supper, we sat around the lawn in deck chairs and drank Sally's beer—it was long before Repeal. We'd repainted the deck chairs ourselves the Sunday before and we felt pretty proud of them. The light stayed late, but there was a breeze after dark, and once Bud started yipping and Sally went up to him. She had on a white dress, I think—she used to wear white a lot in the summers—it went with her blue eyes and her yellow hair. Well, it wasn't anything extraordinary—we didn't even stay up late. But we were all there. And if you'd told me that within three years we'd both be married to other people, I'd have thought you were raving.

Then you went West, remember, and we saw you off on the train. So you didn't see what happened, and, as a matter of fact, it's hard to remember when we first started meeting the Blakes. They'd moved to Meadowfield then, but we hadn't met them.

Jim Blake was one of those pleasant, ugly-faced people with steel glasses who get right ahead in the law and never look young or old. And Lisa was Lisa. She's dark, you know, and she takes a beautiful burn. She was the first girl there to wear real beach things or drink a special kind of tomato juice when everybody else was drinking cocktails. She was very pretty and very good fun to be with—she's got lots of ideas. They entertained a good deal because Lisa likes that—she had her own income, of course. And she and Jim used to bicker a good deal in public in an amusing way—it was sort of an act or seemed like it. They had one little girl, Sylvia, that Jim was crazy about. I mean it sounds normal, doesn't it, even to their having the kind of Airedale you had then? Well, it all seemed normal enough to us, and they got to be part of the crowd. You know, the young married crowd in every suburb.

Of course, that was '28, and the boom was booming and everybody was feeling pretty high. I suppose that was part of it—the money—and the feeling you had that everything was going faster and faster and wouldn't stop. Why, it was Sally herself who said that we owed ourselves a whirl and mustn't get stodgy and settled while we were still young. Well, we had stuck pretty close to the grindstone for the past few years, with the children and everything. And it was fun to feel young and sprightly again and buy a new car and take in the club gala without having to worry about how you'd pay your house account. But I don't see any harm in that.

And then, of course, we talked and kidded a lot about freedom and what have you. Oh, you know the kind of talk—everybody was talking it then. About not being Victorians and living your own life. And there was the older generation and the younger generation. I've forgotten a lot of it now, but I remember there was one piece about love not being just a form of words mumbled by a minister, but something pretty special. As a matter of fact, the minister who married us was old Doctor Snell, and he had the kind of voice you could hear in the next county. But I used to talk about that mumbling minister myself. I mean, we were enlightened, for a suburb, if you get my point. Yes, and pretty proud of it, too. When they banned a book in Boston, the lending library ordered six extra copies. And I still remember the big discussion we had about perfect freedom in marriage when even the straight Republicans voted the radical ticket. All except Chick Bewleigh, and he was a queer, independent sort of bird, who didn't even believe that stocks had reached a permanently high plateau.

But, meanwhile, most of us were getting the 8.15 and our wives were going down to the chain store and asking if that was a really nice head of lettuce. At least that's the way we seemed. And, if the crowd started kidding me about Mary Sennett, or MacChurch kissed Sally on the ear at a club revel, why, we were young, we were modern, and we could handle that. I wasn't going to take a shotgun to Mac, and Sally wasn't going to put on the jealous act. Oh, we had it all down to a science. We certainly did.

Good Lord, we had the Blakes to dinner, and they had us. They'd drop over for drinks or we'd drop over there. It was all perfectly normal and part of the crowd. For that matter, Sally played with Jim Blake in the mixed handicap and they got to the semi-finals. No, I didn't play with Lisa —she doesn't like golf. I mean that's the way it was.

And I can remember the minute it started, and it wasn't anything, just a party at the Bewleighs'. They've got a big, rambling house and people drift around. Lisa and I had wandered out to the kitchen to get some drinks for the people on the porch. She had on a black dress, that night, with a big sort of orange flower on it. It wouldn't have suited everybody, but it suited her.

We were talking along like anybody and suddenly we stopped talking and looked at each other. And I felt, for a minute, well, just the way I felt when I was first in love with Sally. Only this time, it wasn't Sally. It happened so suddenly that all I could think of was: "Watch your step!" Just as if you'd gone into a room in the dark and hit your elbow. I guess that makes it genuine, doesn't it?

We picked it up right away and went back to the party. All she said was: "Did anybody ever tell you that you're really quite a menace, Dan?" and she said that in the way we all said those things. But, all the same, it had happened. I could hear her voice all the way back in the car. And yet, I was as fond of Sally as ever. I don't suppose you'll believe that, but it's true.

And next morning, I tried to kid myself that it didn't have any importance. Because Sally wasn't jealous, and we were all modern and advanced and knew about life. But the next time I saw Lisa, I knew it had.

I want to say this. If you think it was all romance and rosebuds, you're wrong. A lot of it was merry hell. And yet, everybody whooped us on, that's what I don't understand. They didn't really want the Painters and the Blakes to get divorced, and yet they were pretty interested. Now, why do people do that? Some of them would carefully put Lisa and me next to each other at table and some of them would just as carefully not. But it all added up to the same thing in the end—a circus was going on and we were part of the circus. It's interesting to watch the people on the high wires at the circus, and you hope they don't fall. But, if they did, that would be interesting too. Of course, there were a couple of people who tried, as they say, to warn us. But they were older people and just made us mad.

Everybody was so nice and considerate and understanding. Everybody was so nice and intelligent and fine. Don't misunderstand me. It was wonderful, being with Lisa. It was new and exciting. And it seemed to be wonderful for her, and she'd been unhappy with Jim. So, anyway, that made me feel less of a heel, though I felt enough of a

43

heel, from time to time. And then, when we were together, it would seem so fine.

A couple of times we really tried to break it, too—at least twice. But we all belonged to the same crowd, and what could you do but run away? And, somehow, that meant more than running away—it meant giving in to the Victorians and that mumbling preacher and all the things we'd said we didn't believe in. Or I suppose Sally might have done like old Mrs. Pierce, back home. She horsewhipped the dressmaker on the station platform and then threw herself crying into Major Pierce's arms and he took her to Atlantic City instead. It's one of the town's great stories and I always wondered what they talked about on the train. Of course, they moved to Des Moines after that—I remember reading about their golden wedding anniversary when I was in college. Only nobody could do that nowadays, and, besides, Lisa wasn't a dressmaker.

So, finally, one day I came home, and there was Sally, perfectly cold, and we talked pretty nearly all night. We'd been awfully polite to each other for quite a while before—the way you are. And we kept polite, we kept a good grip on ourselves. After all we'd said to each other before we were married that if either of us ever—and there it was. And it was Sally who brought that up, not me. I think we'd have felt better if we'd fought. But we didn't fight.

Of course, she was bound to say some things about Lisa, and I was bound to answer. But that didn't last long and we got our grip right back again. It was funny, being strangers and talking so politely, but we did it. I think it gave us a queer kind of pride to do it. I think it gave us a queer kind of pride for her to ask me politely for a drink at the end, as if she were in somebody else's house, and for me to mix it for her, as if she were a guest.

Everything was talked out by then and the house felt very dry and empty, as if nobody lived in it at all. We'd never been up quite so late in the house, except after a New Year's party or when Buddy was sick, that time. I mixed her drink very carefully, the way she liked it, with plain water, and she took it and said "Thanks." Then she sat for a while without saying anything. It was so quiet you could hear the little drip of the leaky faucet in the pantry, in spite of the door being closed. She heard it and said: "It's dripping again. You better call up Mr. Vye in the morning—I forgot. And I think Barbara's getting a cold— I meant to tell you." Then her face twisted and I thought she was going to cry, but she didn't.

She put the glass down—she'd only drunk half her drink —and said, quite quietly: "Oh, damn you, and damn Lisa Blake, and damn everything in the world!" Then she ran upstairs before I could stop her and she still wasn't crying.

I could have run upstairs after her, but I didn't. I stood looking at the glass on the table and I couldn't think. Then, after a while, I heard a key turn in a lock. So I picked up my hat and went out for a walk—I hadn't been out walking that early in a long time. Finally, I found an all-night café and got some coffee. Then I came back and read a book till the maid got down—it wasn't a very interesting book. When she came down, I pretended I'd gotten up early and had to go into town by the first train, but I guess she knew.

I'm not going to talk about the details. If you've been through them, you've been through them; and if you haven't, you don't know. My family was fond of Sally, and Sally's had always liked me. Well, that made it tough. And the children. They don't say the things you expect them to. I'm not going to talk about that.

Oh, we put on a good act, we put on a great show! There weren't any fists flying or accusations. Everybody said how well we did it, everybody in town. And Lisa and Sally saw each other, and Jim Blake and I talked perfectly calm. We said all the usual things. He talked just as if it were a case. I admired him for it. Lisa did her best to make it emotional, but we wouldn't let her. And I finally made her see that, court or no court, he'd simply have to have Sylvia. He was crazy about her, and while Lisa's a very good mother, there wasn't any question as to which of them the kid liked best. It happens that way, sometimes.

For that matter, I saw Sally off on the train to Reno. She wanted it that way. Lisa was going to get a Mexican divorce—they'd just come in, you know. And nobody could have told, from the way we talked in the station. It's funny, you get a queer bond, through a time like that. After I'd seen her off—and she looked small in the train—the first person I wanted to see wasn't Lisa, but Jim Blake. You see, other people are fine, but unless you've been through things yourself, you don't quite understand them. But Jim Blake was still in Meadowfield, so I went back to the Club.

I hadn't ever really lived in the club before, except for three days one summer. They treat you very well, but, of course, being a college club, it's more for the youngsters and the few old boys who hang around the bar. I got awfully tired of the summer chintz in the dining-room and the Greek waiter I had who breathed on my neck. And you can't work all the time, though I used to stay late at the office. I guess it was then I first thought of getting out of Spencer Wilde and making a new connection. You think about a lot of things at a time like that.

Of course, there were lots of people I could have seen, but I didn't much want to—somehow, you don't. Though I did strike up quite a friendship with one of the old boys. He was about fifty-five and he'd been divorced four times and was living permanently at the club. We used to sit up in his little room—he'd had his own furniture moved in and the walls were covered with pictures—drinking Tom Collinses and talking about life. He had lots of ideas about life, and about matrimony, too, and I got quite interested, listening to him. But then he'd go into the dinners he used to give at Delmonico's, and while that was interesting, too, it wasn't much help, except to take your mind off the summer chintz.

He had some sort of small job, downtown, but I guess he had an income from his family too. He must have. But when I'd ask him what he did, he'd always say: "I'm retired, my boy, very much retired, and how about a touch more beverage to keep out the sun?" He always called it beverage, but they knew what he meant at the bar. He turned up at the wedding, when Lisa and I were married, all dressed up in a cutaway, and insisted on making us a little speech—very nice it was too. Then we had him to dinner a couple of times, after we'd got back, and somehow or other, I haven't seen him since. I suppose he's still at the club—I've got out of the habit of going there, since I joined the other ones, though I still keep my membership.

Of course, all that time, I was crazy about Lisa and writing her letters and waiting till we could be married. Of course I was. But, now and then, even that would get shoved into the background. Because there was so much to do and arrangements to make and people like lawyers to see. I don't like lawyers very much, even yet, though the people we had were very good. But there was all the telephoning and the conferences. Somehow, it was like a machine—a big machine—and you had to learn a sort of new etiquette for everything you did. Till, finally, it got so that about all you wanted was to have the fuss over and not talk about it any more.

I remember running into Chick Bewleigh in the club, three days before Sally got her decree. You'd like Chick—he's the intellectual type, but a darn good fellow too. And Nan, his wife, is a peach—one of those big, rangy girls with a crazy sense of humour. It was nice to talk to him because he was natural and didn't make any cracks about grass-bachelors or get that look in his eye. You know the look they get. We talked about Meadowfield—just the usual news—the Bakers were splitting up and Don Sikes had a new job and the Wilsons were having a baby. But it seemed good to hear it.

"For that matter," he said, drawing on his pipe, "we're adding to the population again ourselves. In the fall. How we'll ever manage four of them! I keep telling Nan she's cock-eyed, but she says they're more fun than a swimming pool and cost less to keep up, so what can you do!"

He shook his head and I remembered that Sally always used to say she wanted six. Only now it would be Lisa, so I mustn't think about that.

"So that's your recipe for a happy marriage," I said. "Well, I always wondered."

I was kidding, of course, but he looked quite serious.

" *Kinder, Küchen und Kirche?*" he said. "Nope, that doesn't work any more, what with pre-schools, automats and the movies. Four children or no four children, Nan could still raise hell if she felt like raising hell. And so could I, for that matter. Add blessings of civilization," and his eyes twinkled.

"Well, then," I said, "what is it?" I really wanted to know.

"Oh, just bull luck, I suppose. And happening to like what you've got," he answered, in a sort of embarrassed way.

"You can do that," I said. "And yet——"

He looked away from me.

"Oh, it was a lot simpler in the old days," he said. "Everything was for marriage—church, laws, society. And when people got married, they expected to stay that way. And it made a lot of people as unhappy as hell. Now the expectation's rather the other way, at least in this great and beautiful nation and among people like us. If you get a divorce, it's rather like going to the dentist—unpleasant sometimes, but lots of people have been there before. Well, that's a handsome system, too, but it's got its own casualty list. So there you are. You takes your money and you makes your choice. And some of us like freedom better than the institution and some of us like the institution better, but what most of us would like is to be Don Juan on Thursdays and Benedict, the married man, on Fridays, Saturdays and the rest of the week. Only that's a bit hard to work out, somehow," and he grinned.

"All the same," I said, "you and Nan——"

"Well," he said, "I suppose we're exceptions. You see, my parents weren't married till I was seven. So I'm a conservative. It might have worked out the other way."

"Oh," I said.

"Yes," he said. "My mother was English, and you may have heard of English divorce laws. She ran away with my father and she was perfectly right—her husband was a very extensive brute. All the same, I was brought up on the other side of the fence, and I know something about what it's like. And Nan was a minister's daughter who thought she ought to be free. Well, we argued about things a good deal. And, finally, I told her that I'd be very highly complimented to live with her on any terms at all, but if she wanted to get married, she'd have to expect a marriage, not a trip to Coney Island. And I made my point rather clear by blacking her eye, in a taxi, when she told me she was thinking seriously of spending a week-end with my deadly rival, just to see which one of us she really loved. You can't spend a romantic week-end with somebody when you've got a black eye. But you can get married with one and we did. She had raw beefsteak on it till two hours before the wedding, and it was the prettiest sight I ever saw. Well, that's our simple story."

"Not all of it," I said.

"No," he said, "not all of it. But at least we didn't start in with any of this bunk about if you meet a handsomer fellow it's all off. We knew we were getting into something. Bewleigh's Easy Guide to Marriage in three instalments—you are now listening to the Voice of Experience, and who cares? Of course, if we hadn't—ahem—liked each other, I could have blacked her eye till Doomsday and got nothing out of it but a suit for assault and battery. But nothing's much good unless it's worth fighting for. And she doesn't look exactly like a downtrodden wife."

"Nope," I said, "but all the same——"

He stared at me very hard—almost the way he used to when people were explaining that stocks had reached a permanently high plateau.

"Exactly," he said. "And there comes a time, no matter what the intention, when a new face heaves into view and a spark lights. I'm no Adonis, God knows, but it's happened to me once or twice. And I know what I do then. I run. I run like a rabbit. It isn't courageous or adventurous or fine. It isn't even particularly moral, as I think about morals. But I run. Because, when all's said and done, it takes two people to make a love affair and you can't have it when one of them's not there. And, dammit, Nan knows it, that's the trouble. She'd ask Helen of Troy to dinner just to see me run. Well, good-bye, old man, and our best to Lisa, of course——"

After he was gone, I went and had dinner in the grill. I did a lot of thinking at dinner, but it didn't get me anywhere. When I was back in the room, I took the receiver off the telephone. I was going to call long distance. But your voice sounds different on the 'phone, and, anyway, the decree would be granted in three days. So when the girl answered, I told her it was a mistake.

Next week Lisa came back and she and I were married. We went to Bermuda on our wedding trip. It's a very pretty place. Do you know, they won't allow an automobile on the island?

The queer thing was that at first I didn't feel married to Lisa at all. I mean, on the boat, and even at the hotel. She said: "But how exciting, darling!" and I suppose it was.

Now, of course, we've been married eight years, and that's always different. The twins will be seven in May— two years older than Sally's Jerry. I had an idea for a while that Sally might marry Jim Blake—he always admired her. But I'm glad she didn't—it would have made things a little too complicated. And I like McConaghey—I like him fine. We gave them an old Chinese jar for a wedding present. Lisa picked it out. She has very good taste and Sally wrote us a fine letter.

I'd like to have you meet Lisa some time—she's interested in intelligent people. They're always coming to the apartment—artists and writers and people like that.

Of course, they don't always turn out the way she expects. But she's quite a hostess and she knows how to handle things. There was one youngster that used to rather get in my hair. He'd call me the Man of Wall Street and ask me what I thought about Picabia or one of those birds, in a way that sort of said: "Now watch this guy stumble!" But as soon as Lisa noticed it, she got rid of him. That shows she's considerate.

Of course, it's different, being married to a person. And I'm pretty busy these days and so is she. Sometimes, if I get home and there's going to be a party, I'll just say good night to the twins and fade out after dinner. But Lisa understands about that, and I've got my own quarters. She had one of her decorator friends do the private study and it really looks very nice.

I had Jim Blake in there one night. Well, I had to take him somewhere. He was getting pretty noisy and Lisa gave me the high sign. He's doing very well, but he looks pretty hard these days and I'm afraid he's drinking a good deal, though he doesn't often show it. I don't think he ever quite got over Sylvia's dying. Four years ago. They had scarlet fever at the school. It was a great shock to Lisa too, of course, but she had the twins and Jim never married again. But he comes to see us, every once in a while. Once, when he was tight, he said it was to convince himself about remaining a bachelor, but I don't think he meant that.

Now, when I brought him into the study, he looked around and said: "Shades of Buck Rogers! What one of Lisa's little dears produced this imitation Wellsian nightmare?"

"Oh, I don't remember," I said. "I think his name was Slivovitz."

"It looks as if it had been designed by a man named Slivovitz," he said. "All dental steel and black glass. I recognize the Lisa touch. You're lucky she didn't put murals of cogwheels on the walls."

"Well, there was a question of that," I said.

"I bet there was," he said. "Well, here's how, old man! Here's to two great big wonderful institutions, marriage and divorce!"

I didn't like that very much and told him so. But he just wagged his head at me.

"I like you, Painter," he said. "I always did. Sometimes I think you're goofy, but I like you. You can't insult me—I won't let you. And it isn't your fault."

"What isn't my fault?" I said.

"The set-up," he said. "Because, in your simple little heart, you're an honest monogamous man, Painter—monogamous as most. And if you'd stayed married to Sally, you'd have led an honest monogamous life. But they loaded the dice against you, out at Meadowfield, and now Lord knows where you'll end up. After all, I was married to Lisa myself for six years or so. Tell me, isn't it hell?"

"You're drunk," I said.

"*In vino veritas*," said he. "No, it isn't hell—I take that back. Lisa's got her damn-fool side, but she's an attractive and interesting woman—or could be, if she'd work at it.

But she was brought up on the idea of Romance with a big R, and she's too bone-lazy and bone-selfish to work at it very long. There's always something else, just over the horizon. Well, I got tired of fighting that, after a while. And so will you. She doesn't want husbands—she wants clients and followers. Or maybe you're tired already."

"I think you'd better go home, Jim," I said. "I don't want to have to ask you."

"Sorry," he said. "*In vino veritas.* But it's a funny set-up, isn't it? What Lisa wanted was a romantic escapade—and she got twins. And what you wanted was marriage—and you got Lisa. As for me," and for a minute his face didn't look drunk any more, "what I principally wanted was Sylvia and I've lost that. I could have married again, but I didn't think that'd be good for her. Now, I'll probably marry some client I've helped with her decree—we don't touch divorce, as a rule, just a very, very special line of business for a few important patrons. I know those—I've had them in the office. And won't that be fun for us all! What a set-up it is!" and he slumped down in his chair and went to sleep. I let him sleep for a while and then had Briggs take him down in the other elevator. He called up next day and apologised—said he knew he must have been noisy, though he couldn't remember anything he said.

The other time I had somebody in the study was when Sally came back there once, two years ago. We'd met to talk about college for Barbara and I'd forgotten some papers I wanted to show her. We generally meet downtown. But she didn't mind coming back—Lisa was out, as it happened. It made me feel queer, taking her up in the elevator and letting her in at the door. She wasn't like Jim—she thought the study was nice.

Well, we talked over our business and I kept looking at her. You can see she's older, but her eyes are still that very bright blue, and she bites her thumb when she's interested. It's a queer feeling. Of course, I was used to seeing her, but we usually met downtown. You know, I wouldn't have been a bit surprised if she'd pushed the bell and said: "Tea, Briggs. I'm home." She didn't, naturally.

I asked her, once, if she wouldn't take off her hat and

she looked at me in a queer way and said: "So you can show me your etchings? Dan, Dan, you're a dangerous man!" and for a moment we both laughed like fools.

"Oh, dear," she said, drying her eyes, "that's very funny. And now I must be going home."

"Look here, Sally," I said, "I've always told you—but, honestly, if you need anything—if there's anything——"

"Of course, Dan," she said. "And we're awfully good friends, aren't we?" But she was still smiling.

I didn't care. "Friends!" I said. "You know how I think about you. I always have. And I don't want you to think——"

She patted my shoulder—I'd forgotten the way she used to do that.

"There," she said. "Mother knows all about it. And we really are friends, Dan. So——"

"I was a fool."

She looked at me very steadily out of those eyes.

"We were all fools," she said. "Even Lisa. I used to hate her for a while. I used to hope things would happen to her. Oh, not very bad things. Just her finding out that you never see a crooked picture without straightening it, and hearing you say: 'A bird can't fly on one wing,' for the dozenth time. The little things everybody has to find out and put up with. But I don't even do that any more."

"If you'd ever learned to put a cork back in a bottle," I said. "I mean the right cork in the right bottle. But——"

"I do so! No, I suppose I never will." And she laughed. She took my hands. "Funny, funny, funny," she said. "And funny to have it all gone and be friends."

"Is it all gone?" I said.

"Why, no, of course not," she said. "I don't suppose it ever is, quite. Like the boys who took you to dances. And there's the children, and you can't help remembering. But it's gone. We had it and lost it. I should have fought for it more, I suppose, but I didn't. And then I was terribly hurt and terribly mad. But I got over that. And now I'm married to Jerry. And I wouldn't give him up, or Jerry Junior, for anything in the world. The only thing that worries me is sometimes when I think it isn't quite a fair deal for him.

53

After all, he could have married—well, somebody else. And yet he knows I love him."

"He ought to," I said rather stiffly. "He's a darn lucky guy, if you ask me."

"No, Dan. I'm the lucky girl. I'm hoping this minute that Mrs. Potter's X-rays turn out all right. He did a beautiful job on her. But he always worries."

I dropped her hands.

"Well, give him my best," I said.

"I will, Dan. He likes you, you know. Really he does. By the way, have you had any more of that bursitis? There's a new treatment—he wanted me to ask you——"

"Thanks," I said, "but that all cleared up."

"I'm glad. And now I must fly. There's always shopping when you come in from the suburbs. Give my best to Lisa and tell her I was sorry not to see her. She's out, I suppose."

"Yes," I said. "She'll be sorry to miss you—you wouldn't stay for a cocktail? She's usually in around then."

"It sounds very dashing, but I mustn't. Jerry Junior lost one of his turtles and I've got to get him another. Do you know a good pet shop? Well, Bloomingdale's, I suppose —after all, I've got other things to get."

"There's a good one two blocks down on Lexington," I said. "But if you're going to Bloomingdale's—well, good-bye, Sally, and good luck."

"Good-bye, Dan. And good luck to you. And no regrets."

"No regrets," I said, and we shook hands.

There wasn't any point in going down to the street with her, and besides I had to 'phone the office. But before I did, I looked out, and she was just getting into a cab. A person looks different, somehow, when they don't know you're seeing them. I could see the way she looked to other people—not young any more, not the Sally I'd married, not even the Sally I'd talked with, all night in that cold house. She was a nice married woman who lived in Montclair and whose husband was a doctor; a nice woman, in shopping for the day, with a new spring hat and a fifty-trip ticket in her handbag. She'd had trouble in her life, but she'd worked it out. And, before she got on the train, she'd have a black-and-white soda, sitting on a stool at the station, or maybe she didn't do that any more. There'd be lots of things in her handbag, but I wouldn't know about any of them nor what locks the keys fitted. And if she were dying, they'd send for me, because that would be etiquette. And the same if I were dying. But we'd have something and lost it—the way she said—and that was all that was left.

Now she was that nice Mrs. McConaghey. But she'd never be quite that to me. And yet, there was no way to go back. You wouldn't even go back to the house in Meadow-field—they'd torn it down and put up an apartment instead.

So that's why I wanted to talk to you. I'm not complaining and I'm not the kind of fellow that gets nerves. But I just want to know—I just want to figure it out. And sometimes it keeps going round and round in your head. You'd like to be able to tell your children something, especially when they're growing up. Well, I know what we'll tell them. But I wonder if it's enough.

Not that we don't get along well when Bud and Barbara come to see us. Especially Barbara—she's very tactful and she's crazy about the twins. And now they're growing up, it's easier. Only, once in a while, something happens that makes you think. I took Barbara out sailing last summer. She's sixteen and a very sweet kid, if I say it myself. A lot of kids that age seem pretty hard, but she isn't.

Well, we were just talking along, and, naturally, you like to know what your children's plans are. Bud thinks he wants to be a doctor like McConaghey and I've no objection. I asked Barbara if she wanted a career, but she said she didn't think so.

"Oh, I'd like to go to college," she said, "and maybe work for a while, afterwards, the way mother did, you know. But I haven't any particular talents, dad. I could kid myself, but I haven't. I guess it's just woman's function and home and babies for me."

"Well, that sounds all right to me," I said, feeling very paternal.

"Yes," she said, "I like babies. In fact, I think I'll get married pretty young, just for the experience. The first time probably won't work, but it ought to teach you some things. And then, eventually, you might find somebody to tie to."

"So that's the way it is with the modern young woman?" I said.

"Why, of course," she said. "That's what practically all the girls say—we've talked it all over at school. Of course, sometimes it takes you quite a while. Like Helen Hastings's mother. She just got married for the fourth time last year, but he really is a sweet! He took us all to the matinée when I was visiting Helen and we nearly died. He's a count, of course, and he's got the darlingest accent. I don't know whether I'd like a count, though it must be fun to have little crowns on your handkerchiefs like Helen's mother. What's the matter, daddy? Are you shocked?"

"Don't flatter yourself, young lady—I've been shocked by experts," I said. "No, I was just thinking. Suppose we— well, suppose your mother and I had stayed together? How would you have felt about it then?"

"But you didn't, did you?" she said, and her voice wasn't hurt or anything, just natural. "I mean, almost nobody does any more. Don't worry, daddy. Bud and I understand all about it—good gracious, we're grown up! Of course, if you and mother had," she said, rather dutifully, "I suppose it would have been very nice. But then we'd have missed Mac, and he really is a sweet, and you'd have missed Lisa and the twins. Anyhow, it's all worked out now. Oh, of course, I'd rather hope it would turn out all right the first time, if it wasn't too stodgy or sinister. But you've got to face facts, you know."

"Face facts!" I said. "Dammit, Barbara!"

Then I stopped, because what did I have to say?

Well, that's the works, and if you've got any dope on it, I wish you'd tell me. There are so few people you can talk to—that's the trouble. I mean everybody's very nice, but that's not the same thing. And, if you start thinking too much, the highballs catch up on you. And you can't afford that—I've never been much of a drinking man.

The only thing is, where does it stop, if it does? That's the thing I'm really afraid of.

It may sound silly to you. But I've seen other people—

well, take this Mrs. Hastings, Barbara talked about. Or my old friend at the club. I wonder if he started in, wanting to get married four times. I know I didn't—I'm not the type and you know it.

And yet, suppose, well, you do meet somebody who treats you like a human being. I mean somebody who doesn't think you're a little goofy because you know more about American Can than who painted what. Supposing, even, they're quite a lot younger. That shouldn't make all the difference. After all, I'm no Lothario. And Lisa and I aren't thinking of a divorce or anything like that. But, naturally, we lead our own lives, and you ought to be able to talk to somebody. Of course, if it could have been Sally. That was my fault. But it isn't as if Maureen were just in the floor show. She's got her own speciality number. And, really, when you get to know her, she's a darned intelligent kid.

DOC MELLHORN HAD NEVER expected to go anywhere at all when he died. So, when he found himself on the road again, it surprised him. But perhaps I'd better explain a little about Doc Mellhorn first. He was seventy-odd when he left our town; but when he came, he was as young as Bates or Filsinger or any of the boys at the hospital. Only there wasn't any hospial when he came. He came with a young man's beard and a brand-new bag and a lot of new-fangled ideas about medicine that we didn't take to much. And he left, forty-odd years later, with a first-class county health record and a lot of people alive that wouldn't have been alive if he hadn't been there. Yes, a country doctor. And nobody ever called him a man in white or a death grappler, that I know of, though they did think of giving him a degree at Pewauket College once. But then the board met again and decided they needed a new gymnasium, so they gave the degree to J. Prentiss Parmalee instead.

They say he was a thin young man when he first came, a thin young man with an Eastern accent who'd wanted to study in Vienna. But most of us remember him chunky and solid, with white hair and a little bald spot that always got burned bright red in the first hot weather. He had about four card tricks that he'd do for you, if you were a youngster —they were always the same ones—and now and then, if he felt like it, he'd take a silver half-dollar out of the back of your neck. And that worked as well with the youngsters who were going to build rocket ships as it had with the youngsters who were going to be railway engineers. It always worked. I guess it was Doc Mellhorn more than the trick.

But there wasn't anything unusual about him, except maybe the card tricks. Or anyway, he didn't think so. He was just a good doctor and he knew us inside out. I've heard people call him a pig-headed, obstinate old mule—that was in the fight about the water supply. And I've heard a weepy old lady call him a saint. I took the tale to him once, and he looked at me over his glasses and said: "Well, I've always respected a mule. Got ten times the sense of a —— horse." Then he took a silver half-dollar out of my ear.

Well, how do you describe a man like that? You don't— you call him up at three in the morning. And when he sends in his bill, you think it's a little steep.

All the same, when it came to it, there were people who drove a hundred and fifty miles to the funeral. And the Masons came down from Bluff City, and the Poles came from across the tracks, with a wreath the size of a house, and you saw cars in town that you didn't often see there. But it was after the funeral that the queer things began for Doc Mellhorn.

The last thing he remembered, he'd been lying in bed, feeling pretty sick, on the whole, but glad for the rest. And now he was driving his Model T down a long straight road between rolling, misty prairies that seemed to go from nowhere to nowhere.

It didn't seem funny to him to be driving the Model T again. That was the car he'd learned on, and he kept to it till his family made him change. And it didn't seem funny to him not to be sick any more. He hadn't had much time to be sick in his life—the patients usually attended to that. He looked around for his bag, first thing, but it was there on the seat beside him. It was the old bag, not the presentation one they'd given him at the hospital, but that was all right too. It meant he was out on a call and, if he couldn't quite recollect at the moment just where the call was, it was certain to come to him. He'd wakened up often enough in his buggy, in the old days, and found the horse was taking him home, without his doing much about it. A doctor gets used to things like that.

All the same, when he'd driven and driven for some time without raising so much as a traffic light, just the same rolling prairies on either hand, he began to get a little suspicious. He thought, for a while, of stopping the car and getting out, just to take a look around, but he'd always hated to lose time on a call. Then he noticed something else. He was driving without his glasses. And yet he hadn't driven without his glasses in fifteen years.

"H'm," said Doc Mellhorn. "I'm crazy as a June bug. Or else—— Well, it might be so, I suppose."

But this time he did stop the car. He opened his bag and looked inside it, but everything seemed to be in order. He opened his wallet and looked at that, but there were his own initials, half rubbed away, and he recognised them. He took his pulse, but it felt perfectly steady.

"H'm," said Doc Mellhorn. "Well."

Then, just to prove that everything was perfectly normal, he took a silver half-dollar out of the steering-wheel of the car.

"Never did it smoother," said Doc Mellhorn. "Well, all the same, if this is the new highway, it's longer than I remember it."

But just then a motor-cycle came roaring down the road and stopped with a flourish, the way motor cops do.

"Any trouble?" said the motor cop. Doc Mellhorn couldn't see his face for the goggles, but the goggles looked normal.

"I am a physician," said Doc Mellhorn, as he'd said a thousand times before to all sorts of people, "on my way to an urgent case." He passed his hand across his forehead. "Is this the right road?" he said.

"Straight ahead to the traffic light," said the cop. "They're expecting you, Doctor Mellhorn. Shall I give you an escort?"

"No; thanks all the same," said Doc Mellhorn, and the motor cop roared away. The Model T ground as Doc Mellhorn gassed her. "Well, they've got a new breed of traffic cop," said Doc Mellhorn, "or else——"

But when he got to the light, it was just like any light at a cross-roads. He waited till it changed and the officer waved him on. There seemed to be a good deal of traffic going the other way, but he didn't get a chance to notice it much, because Lizzie bucked a little, as she usually did when you kept her waiting. Still, the sight of traffic relieved him, though he hadn't passed anybody on his own road yet.

Pretty soon he noticed the look of the country had

changed. It was parkway now and very nicely landscaped. There was dogwood in bloom on the little hills, white and pink against the green; though, as Doc Mellhorn remembered it, it had been August when he left his house. And every now and then there'd be a nice little white-painted sign that said To THE GATES.

"H'm," said Doc Mellhorn. "New State Parkway, I guess. Well, they've fixed it up pretty. But I wonder where they got the dogwood. Haven't seen it bloom like that since I was East."

Then he drove along in a sort of dream for a while, for the dogwood reminded him of the days when he was a young man in an eastern college. He remembered the look of that college and the girls who'd come to dances, the girls who wore white gloves and had rolls of hair. They were pretty girls, too, and he wondered what had become of them. "Had babies, I guess," thought Doc Mellhorn. "Or some of them, anyway." But he liked to think of them as the way they had been when they were just pretty, and excited at being at a dance.

He remembered other things too—the hacked desks in the lecture-rooms, and the trees on the campus, and the first pipe he'd ever broken in, and a fellow called Paisley Grew that he hadn't thought of for years—a raw-boned fellow with a gift for tall stories and playing the jew's-harp.

"Ought to have looked up Paisley," he said. "Yes, I ought. Didn't amount to a hill of beans, I guess, but I always liked him. I wonder if he still plays the jew's-harp. Pshaw, I know he's been dead twenty years."

He was passing other cars now and other cars were passing him, but he didn't pay much attention, except when he happened to notice a licence you didn't often see in the state, like Rhode Island or Mississippi. He was too full of his own thoughts. There were foot passengers, too, plenty of them—and once he passed a man driving a load of hay. He wondered what the man would do with the hay when he got to the Gates. But probably there were arrangements for that.

"Not that I believe a word of it," he said, "but it'll surprise Father Kelly. Or maybe it won't. I used to have some

C

handsome arguments with that man, but I always knew I could count on him, in spite of me being a heretic."

Then he saw the Wall and the Gates, right across the valley. He saw them, and they reached to the top of the sky. He rubbed his eyes for a while, but they kept on being there.

"Quite a sight," said Doc Mellhorn.

No one told him just where to go or how to act, but it seemed to him that he knew. If he'd thought about it, he'd have said that you waited in line, but there wasn't any waiting in line. He just went where he was expected to go and the reception clerk knew his name right away.

"Yes, Doctor Mellhorn," he said. "And now, what would you like to do first?"

"I think I'd like to sit down," said Doc Mellhorn. So he sat, and it was a comfortable chair. He even bounced the springs of it once or twice, till he caught the reception clerk's eye on him.

"If there anything I can get you?" said the reception clerk. He was young and brisk and neat as a pin, and you could see he aimed to give service and studied about it. Doc Mellhorn thought: "He's the kind that wipes off your windshield no matter how clean it is."

"No," said Doc Mellhorn. "You see, I don't believe this. I don't believe any of it. I'm sorry if that sounds cranky, but I don't."

"That's quite all right, sir," said the reception clerk. "It often takes a while." And he smiled as if Doc Mellhorn had done him a favour.

"Young man, I'm a physician," said Doc Mellhorn, "and do you mean to tell me——"

Then he stopped, for he suddenly saw there was no use arguing. He was either there or he wasn't. And it felt as if he were there.

"Well," said Doc Mellhorn, with a sigh, "how do I begin?"

"That's entirely at your own volition, sir," said the reception clerk briskly. "Any meetings with relatives, of course. Or if you would prefer to get yourself settled first. Or take a tour, alone or conducted. Perhaps these will offer suggestions," and he started to hand over a handful of leaflets. But Doc Mellhorn put them aside.

"Wait a minute," he said. "I want to think. Well, naturally, there's Mother and Dad. But I couldn't see them just yet. I wouldn't believe it. And Grandma—well, now, if I saw Grandma—and me older than she is—was—used to be—well, I don't know what it would do to me. You've got to let me get my breath. Well, of course, there's Uncle Frank—he'd be easier." He paused. "Is he here?" he said.

The reception clerk looked in a file. "I am happy to say that Mr. Francis V. Mellhorn arrived July 12, 1907," he said. He smiled winningly.

"Well!" said Doc Mellhorn. "Uncle Frank! Well, I'll be—well! But it must have been a great consolation to Mother. We heard—well, never mind what we heard—I guess it wasn't so. . . . No, don't reach for that phone just yet, or whatever it is. I'm still thinking."

"We sometimes find," said the reception clerk eagerly, "that a person not a relative may be the best introduction. Even a stranger sometimes—a distinguished stranger connected with one's own profession——"

"Well, now, that's an idea," said Doc Mellhorn heartily, trying to keep his mind off how much he disliked the reception clerk. He couldn't just say why he disliked him, but he knew he did.

It reminded him of the time he'd had to have his gall bladder out in the city hospital and the young, brisk interns had come to see him and called him "Doctor" every other word.

"Yes, that's an idea," he said. He reflected. "Well, of course, I'd like to see Koch," he said. "And Semmelweiss. Not to speak of Walter Reed. But, shucks, they'd be busy men. But there is one fellow—only he lived pretty far back——"

"Hippocrates, please," said the reception clerk into the telephone or whatever it was. "*H* for horse——"

"No!" said Doc Mellhorn quite violently. "Excuse me, but you just wait a minute. I mean if you can wait. I mean, if Hippocrates wants to come, I've no objection. But I never took much of a fancy to him, in spite of his oath. It's

63

Aesculapius I'm thinking about. George W. Oh, glory!"
he said. "But he won't talk English. I forgot."

"I shall be happy to act as interpreter," said the reception clerk, smiling brilliantly.

"I haven't a doubt," said Doc Mellhorn. "But just wait
a shake." In a minute, by the way the clerk was acting, he
was going to be talking to Aesculapius. "And what in time
am I going to say to the man?" he thought. "It's too much."
He gazed wildly around the neat reception-room—distempered, as he noticed, in a warm shade of golden tan.
Then his eyes fell on the worn black bag at his feet and a
sudden warm wave of relief flooded over him.

"Wait a minute," he said, and his voice gathered force
and authority. "Where's my patient?"

"Patient?" said the reception clerk, looking puzzled for
the first time.

"Patient," said Doc Mellhorn. "*P* for phlebitis." He
tapped his bag.

"I'm afraid you don't quite understand, sir," said the
reception clerk.

"I understand this," said Doc Mellhorn. "I was called
here. And if I wasn't called professionally, why have I got
my bag?"

"But, my dear Doctor Mellhorn——" said the reception
clerk.

"I'm not your dear doctor," said Doc Mellhorn. "I was
called here, I tell you. I'm sorry not to give you the patient's
name, but the call must have come in my absence and the
girl doesn't spell very well. But in any well-regulated
hospital——"

"But I tell you," said the reception clerk, and his hair
wasn't slick any more, "nobody's ill here. Nobody can be
ill. If they could, it wouldn't be He——"

"Humph," said Doc Mellhorn. He thought it over, and
felt worse. "Then what does a fellow like Koch do?" he
said. "Or Pasteur?" He raised a hand. "Oh, don't tell me,"
he said. "I can see they'd be busy. Yes, I guess it'd be all
right for a research man. But I never was. . . . Oh, well,
shucks, I've published a few papers. And there's that clamp
of mine—always meant to do something about it. But

64

they've got better ones now. Mean to say there isn't so much as a case of mumps in the whole place?"

"I assure you," said the reception clerk, in a weary voice. "And now, once you see Doctor Aesculapius——"

"Funny," said Doc Mellhorn. "Lord knows there's plenty of times you'd be glad to be quit of the whole thing. And don't talk to me about the healer's art or grateful patients. Well, I've known a few . . . a few. But I've known others. All the same, it's different, being told there isn't any need for what you can do."

"*A* for Ararát," said the reception clerk into his instrument. "*E* for Eden."

"Should think you'd have a dial," said Doc Mellhorn desperately. "We've got 'em down below." He thought hard and frantically. "Wait a shake. It's coming back to me," he said. "Got anybody named Grew here? Paisley Grew?"

"*S* for serpent . . ." said the reception clerk. "What was that?"

"Fellow that called me," said Doc Mellhorn. "G-r-e-w. First name, Paisley."

"I will consult the index," said the reception clerk.

He did so, and Doc Mellhorn waited, hoping against hope.

"We have 94,183 Grews, including 83 Prescotts and one Penobscot," the reception clerk said at last. "But I fail to find Paisley Grew. Are you quite sure of the name?"

"Of course," said Doc Mellhorn briskly. "Paisley Grew. Chronic indigestion. Might be appendix—can't say—have to see. But anyhow, he's called." He picked up his bag. "Well, thanks for the information," he said, liking the reception clerk better than he had yet. "Not your fault, anyway."

"But—but where are you going?" said the reception clerk.

"Well, there's another establishment, isn't there?" said Doc Mellhorn. "Always heard there was. Call probably came from there. Crossed wires, I expect."

"But you can't go there!" said the reception clerk. "I mean——"

65

"Can't go?" said Doc Mellhorn. "I'm a physician. A patient's called me."

"But if you'll only wait and see Aesculapius!" said the reception clerk, running his hands wildly through his hair. "He'll be here almost any moment."

"Please give him my apologies," said Doc Mellhorn. "He's a doctor. He'll understand. And if any messages come for me, just stick them on the spike. Do I need a road map? Noticed the road I came was all one way."

"There is, I believe, a back road in rather bad repair," said the reception clerk icily. "I can call Information if you wish."

"Oh, don't bother," said Doc Mellhorn. "I'll find it. And I never saw a road beat Lizzie yet." He took a silver half-dollar from the door-knob of the door. "See that?" he said. "Slick as a whistle. Well, good-bye, young man."

But it wasn't till he'd cranked up Lizzie and was on his way that Doc Mellhorn really felt safe. He found the back road and it was all that the reception clerk had said it was and more. But he didn't mind—in fact, after one particularly bad rut, he grinned.

"I suppose I ought to have seen the folks," he said. "Yes, I know I ought. But—not so much as a case of mumps in the whole abiding dominion! Well, it's lucky I took a chance on Paisley Grew."

After another mile or so, he grinned again.

"And I'd like to see old Aesculapius' face. Probably rang him in the middle of dinner—they always do. But shucks, it's happened to all of us."

Well, the road got worse and worse and the sky above it darker and darker, and what with one thing and another, Doc Mellhorn was glad enough when he got to the other gates. They were pretty impressive gates, too, though of course in a different way, and reminded Doc Mellhorn a little of the furnaces outside Steeltown, where he'd practised for a year when he was young.

This time Doc Mellhorn wasn't going to take any advice from reception clerks and he had his story all ready. All the same, he wasn't either registered or expected, so there was a little fuss. Finally they tried to scare him by saying

66

he came at his own risk and that there were some pretty tough characters about. But Doc Mellhorn remarked that he'd practised in Steeltown. So, after he'd told them what seemed to him a million times that he was a physician on a case, they finally let him in and directed him to Paisley Grew. Paisley was on Level 346 in Pit 68,953, and Doc Mellhorn recognised him the minute he saw him. He even had the jew's-harp stuck in the back of his overalls.

"Well, Doc," said Paisley finally, when the first greetings were over, "you certainly are a sight for sore eyes! Though, of course, I'm sorry to see you here," and he grinned.

"Well, I can't see that it's so different from a lot of places," said Doc Mellhorn, wiping his forehead. "Warmish, though."

"It's the humidity, really," said Paisley Grew. "That's what it really is."

"Yes, I know," said Doc Mellhorn. "And now tell me, Paisley; how's that indigestion of yours?"

"Well, I'll tell you Doc," said Paisley. "When I first came here, I thought the climate was doing it good. I did for a fact. But now I'm not so sure. I've tried all sorts of things for it—I've even tried being transferred to the boiling asphalt lakes. But it just seems to hang on, and every now and then, when I least expect it, it catches me. Take last night. I didn't have a thing to eat that I don't generally eat—well, maybe I did have one little snort of hot sulphur, but it wasn't the sulphur that did it. All the same, I woke up at four, and it was just like a knife. Now . . ."

He went on from there and it took him some time. And Doc Mellhorn listened, happy as a clam. He never thought he'd be glad to listen to a hypochondriac, but he was. And when Paisley was all through, he examined him and prescribed for him. It was just a little soda bicarb and pepsin, but Paisley said it took hold something wonderful. And they had a fine time that evening, talking over the old days.

Finally, of course, the talk got around to how Paisley liked it where he was. And Paisley was honest enough about that.

"Well, Doc," he said, "of course this isn't the place for you, and I can see you're just visiting. But I haven't many

67

real complaints. It's hot, to be sure, and they work you, and some of the boys here are rough. But they've had some pretty interesting experiences too, when you get them talking—yes, sir. And anyhow, it isn't Peabodyville, New Jersey," he said with vehemence. "I spent five years in Peabodyville, trying to work up in the leather business. After that I bust out, and I guess that's what landed me here. But it's an improvement on Peabodyville." He looked at Doc Mellhorn sidewise. "Say, Doc," he said, "I know this is a vacation for you, but all the same there's a couple of the boys—nothing really wrong with them of course—but—well, if you could just look them over——"

"I was thinking the office hours would be nine to one," said Doc Mellhorn.

So Paisley took him around and they found a nice little place for an office in one of the abandoned mine galleries, and Doc Mellhorn hung out his shingle. And right away patients started coming around. They didn't get many doctors there, in the first place, and the ones they did get weren't exactly the cream of the profession, so Doc Mellhorn had it all to himself. It was mostly sprains, fractures, bruises and dislocations, of course, with occasional burns and scalds—and, on the whole, it reminded Doc Mellhorn a good deal of his practice in Steeltown, especially when it came to foreign bodies in the eye. Now and then Doc Mellhorn ran into a more unusual case—for instance, there was one of the guards that got part of himself pretty badly damaged in a rock slide. Well, Doc Mellhorn had never set a tail before, but he managed it all right, and got a beautiful primary union, too, in spite of the fact that he had no X-ray facilities. He thought of writing up the case for the State Medical Journal, but then he couldn't figure out any way to send it to them, so he had to let it slide. And then there was an advanced carcinoma of the liver—a Greek named Papadoupolous or Prometheus or something. Doc Mellhorn couldn't do much for him, considering the circumstances, but he did what he could, and he and the Greek used to have long conversations. The rest was just everyday practice —run of the mine—but he enjoyed it.

Now and then it would cross his mind that he ought to

get out Lizzie and run back to the other place for a visit with the folks. But that was just like going back East had been on earth—he'd think he had everything pretty well cleared up, and then a new flock of patients would come in. And it wasn't that he didn't miss his wife and children and grandchildren—he did. But there wasn't any way to get back to them, and he knew it. And there was the work in front of him and the office crowded every day. So he just went along, hardly noticing the time.

Now and then, to be sure, he'd get a suspicion that he wasn't too popular with the authorities of the place. But he was used to not being popular with authorities and he didn't pay much attention. But finally they sent an inspector round. The minute Doc Mellhorn saw him, he knew there was going to be trouble.

Not that the inspector was uncivil. In fact, he was a pretty high-up official—you could tell by his antlers. And Doc Mellhorn was just as polite, showing him round. He showed him the free dispensary and the clinic and the nurse —Scotch girl named Smith, she was—and the dental chair he'd rigged up with the help of a fellow named Ferguson, who used to be an engineer before he was sentenced. And the inspector looked them all over, and finally he came back to Doc Mellhorn's office. The girl named Smith had put up curtains in the office, and with that and a couple of potted gas plants it looked more home-like than it had. The inspector looked around it and sighed.

"I'm sorry, Doctor Mellhorn," he said at last, "but you can see for yourself, it won't do."

"What won't do?" said Doc Mellhorn, stoutly. But, all the same, he felt afraid.

"Any of it," said the inspector. "We could overlook the alleviation of minor suffering—I'd be inclined to do so myself—though these people are here to suffer, and there's no changing that. But you're playing merry Hades with the whole system."

"I'm a physician in practice," said Doc Mellhorn.

"Yes," said the inspector. "That's just the trouble. Now, take these reports you've been sending," and he took out a sheaf of papers. "What have you to say about that?"

69

CI

"Well, seeing as there's no county health officer, or at least I couldn't find one——" said Doc Mellhorn.

"Precisely," said the inspector. "And what have you done? You've condemned fourteen levels of this pit as unsanitary nuisances. You've recommended 2,136 lost souls for special diet, remedial exercise, hospitalisation—— Well —I won't go through the list."

"I'll stand back of every one of those recommendations," said Doc Mellhorn. "And now we've got the chair working, we can handle most of the dental work on the spot. Only Ferguson needs more amalgam."

"I know," said the inspector patiently, "but the money has to come from somewhere—you must realise that. We're not a rich community, in spite of what people think. And these unauthorised requests—oh, we fill them, of course, but——"

"Ferguson needs more amalgam," said Doc Mellhorn. "And that last batch wasn't standard. I wouldn't use it on a dog."

"He's always needing more amalgam!" said the inspector bitterly, making a note. "Is he going to fill every tooth in Hades? By the way, my wife tells me I need a little work done myself—but we won't go into that. We'll take just one thing—your entirely unauthorised employment of Miss Smith. Miss Smith has no business working for you. She's supposed to be gnawed by a never-dying worm every Monday, Wednesday and Friday."

"Sounds silly to me," said Doc Mellhorn.

"I don't care how silly it sounds," said the inspector. "It's regulations. And, besides, she isn't even a registered nurse."

"She's a practical one," said Doc Mellhorn. "Of course, back on earth a lot of her patients died. But that was because when she didn't like a patient she poisoned him. Well, she can't poison anybody here and I've kind of got her out of the notion of it anyway. She's been doing A-1 work for me and I'd like to recommend her for——"

"Please!" said the inspector. "Please! And as if that wasn't enough, you've even been meddling with the staff. I've a note here on young Asmodeus—Asmodeus XIV——"

"Oh, you mean Mickey!" said Doc Mellhorn, with a chuckle. "Short for Mickey Mouse. We call him that in the clinic. And he's a young imp if ever I saw one."

"The original Asmodeus is one of our most prominent citizens," said the inspector severely. "How do you suppose he felt when we got your report that his fourteenth great-grandson had rickets?"

"Well," said Doc Mellhorn, "I know rickets. And he had 'em. And you're going to have rickets in these youngsters as long as you keep feeding 'em low-grade coke. I put Mickey on the best Pennsylvania anthracite, and look at him now!"

"I admit the success of your treatment," said the inspector, "but, naturally—well, since then we've been deluged with demands for anthracite from as far south as Sheol. We'll have to float a new bond issue. And what will the taxpayers say?"

"He was just cutting his first horns when he came to us," said Doc Mellhorn reminiscently, "and they were coming in crooked. Now, I ask you, did you ever see a straighter pair? Of course, if I'd had cod liver oil—— My gracious, you ought to have somebody here that can fill a prescription; I can't do it all."

The inspector shut his papers together with a snap. "I'm sorry, Doctor Mellhorn," he said, "but this is final. You have no right here, in the first place; no local licence to practise in the second——"

"Yes, that's a little irregular," said Doc Mellhorn, "but I'm a registered member of four different medical associations—you might take that into account. And I'll take any examination that's required."

"No," said the inspector violently. "No, no, no! You can't stay here! You've got to go away! It isn't possible!"

Doc Mellhorn drew a long breath. "Well," he said, "there wasn't any work for me at the other place. And here you won't let me practise. So what's a man to do?"

The inspector was silent.

"Tell me," said Doc Mellhorn presently. "Suppose you do throw me out? What happens to Miss Smith and Paisley and the rest of them?"

"Oh, what's done is done," said the inspector impatiently, "here as well as anywhere else. We'll have to keep on with the anthracite and the rest of it. And Hades only knows what'll happen in the future. If it's any satisfaction to you, you've started something."

"Well, I guess Smith and Ferguson between them can handle the practice," said Doc Mellhorn. "But that's got to be a promise."

"It's a promise," said the inspector.

"Then there's Mickey—I mean Asmodeus," said Doc Mellhorn. "He's a smart youngster—smart as a whip—if he is a hellion. Well, you know how a youngster gets. Well, it seems he wants to be a doctor. But I don't know what sort of training he'd get——"

"He'll get it," said the inspector feverishly. "We'll found the finest medical college you ever saw, right here in West Baal. We'll build a hospital that'll knock your eye out. You'll be satisfied. But now, if you don't mind——"

"All right," said Doc Mellhorn, and rose.

The inspector looked surprised. "But don't you want to——" he said. "I mean my instructions are we're to give you a banquet, if necessary—after all, the community appreciates——"

"Thanks," said Doc Mellhorn, with a shudder, "but if I've got to go, I'd rather get out of town. You hang around and announce your retirement, and pretty soon folks start thinking they ought to give you a testimonial. And I never did like testimonials."

All the same, before he left he took a silver half-dollar out of Mickey Asmodeus' chin.

When he was back on the road again and the lights of the gates had faded into a low ruddy glow behind him, Doc Mellhorn felt alone for the first time. He'd been lonely at times during his life, but he'd never felt alone like this before. Because, as far as he could see, there was only him and Lizzie now.

"Now, maybe if I'd talked to Aesculapius —" he said. "But pshaw, I always was pig-headed."

He didn't pay much attention to the way he was driving and it seemed to him that the road wasn't quite the same.

But he felt tired for a wonder—bone-tired and beaten—and he didn't much care about the road. He hadn't felt tired since he left earth, but now the loneliness tired him.

"Active—always been active," he said to himself. "I can't just lay down on the job. But what's a man to do?"

"What's a man to do?" he said. "I'm a doctor. I can't work miracles."

Then the black fit came over him and he remembered all the times he'd been wrong and all the people he couldn't do anything for. "Never was much of a doctor, I guess," he said. "Maybe, if I'd gone to Vienna. Well, the right kind of man would have gone. And about that Bigelow kid," he said. "How was I to know he'd haemorrhage? But I should have known.

"I've diagnosed walking typhoid as appendicitis. Just the once, but that's enough. And I still don't know what held me back when I was all ready to operate. I used to wake up in a sweat, six months afterward, thinking I had.

"I could have saved those premature twins, if I'd known as much then as I do now. I guess that guy Dafoe would have done it anyway—look at what he had to work with. But I didn't. And that finished the Gorhams' having children. That's a dandy doctor, isn't it? Makes you feel fine.

"I could have pulled Old Man Halsey through. And Edna Biggs. And the little Lauriat girl. No, I couldn't have done it with her. That was before insulin. I couldn't have cured Ted Allen. No, I'm clear on that. But I've never been satisfied about the Collins woman. Bates is all right—good as they come. But I knew her, inside and out—ought to, too—she was the biggest nuisance that ever came into the office. And if I hadn't been down with the 'flu . . .

"Then there's the 'flu epidemic. I didn't take my clothes off, four days and nights. But what's the good of that, when you lose them? Oh, sure, the statistics looked good. You can have the statistics.

"Should have started raising hell about the water supply two years before I did.

"Oh, yes, it makes you feel fine, pulling babies into the world. Makes you feel you're doing something. And just

73

fine when you see a few of them, twenty-thirty years later, not worth two toots on a cow's horn. Can't say I ever delivered a Dillinger. But there's one or two in state's prison. And more that ought to be. Don't mind even that so much as a few of the fools. Makes you wonder.

"And then, there's incurable cancer. That's a daisy. What can you do about it, Doctor? Well, Doctor, we can alleviate the pain in the last stages. Some. Ever been in a cancer ward, Doctor? Yes, Doctor, I have.

"What do you do for the common cold, Doctor? Two dozen clean linen handkerchiefs. Yes, it's a good joke—I'll laugh. And what do you do for a boy when you know he's dying, Doctor? Take a silver half-dollar out of his ear. But it kept the Lane kid quiet and his fever went down that night. I took the credit, but I don't know why it went down.

"I've only got one brain. And one pair of hands.

"I could have saved. I could have done. I could have.

"Guess it's just as well you can't live for ever. You make fewer mistakes. And sometimes I'd see Bates looking at me as if he wondered why I ever thought I could practise.

"Pig-headed, opinionated, ineffective old imbecile! And yet, Lord, Lord, I'd do it all over again."

He lifted his eyes from the pattern of the road in front of him. There were white markers on it now, and Lizzie seemed to be bouncing down a residential street. There were trees in the street and it reminded him of town. He rubbed his eyes for a second, and Lizzie rolled on by herself—she often did. It didn't seem strange to him to stop at the right house.

"Well, Mother," he said rather gruffly to the group on the lawn. "Well, Dad. . . . Well, Uncle Frank." He beheld a small, stern figure advancing, hands outstretched. "Well, Grandma," he said meekly.

Later on he was walking up and down in the grape arbour with Uncle Frank. Now and then he picked a grape and ate it. They'd always been good grapes, those Catawbas, as he remembered them.

"What beats me," he said, not for the first time, "is why I didn't notice the Gates. The second time, I mean."

"Oh, that Gate," said Uncle Frank, with the easy, unctuous roll in his voice that Doc Mellhorn so well remembered. He smoothed his handle-bar moustaches. "That Gate, my dear Edward—well, of course it has to be there in the first place. Literature, you know. And then, it's a choice," he said richly.

"I'll draw cards," said Doc Mellhorn. He ate another grape.

"Fact is," said Uncle Frank, "that Gate's for one kind of person. You pass it and then you can rest for all eternity. Just fold your hands. It suits some."

"I can see that it would," said Doc Mellhorn.

"Yes," said Uncle Frank, "but it wouldn't suit a Mellhorn. I'm happy to say that very few of our family remain permanently on that side. I spent some time there myself." He said, rather self-consciously: "Well, my last years had been somewhat stormy. So few people cared for refined impersonations of our feathered songsters, including lightning sketches. I felt that I'd earned a rest. But after a while—well, I got tired of being at liberty."

"And what happens when you get tired?" said Doc Mellhorn.

"You find out what you want to do," said Uncle Frank.

"My kind of work?" said Doc Mellhorn.

"Your kind of work," said his uncle. "Been busy, haven't you?"

"Well," said Doc Mellhorn. "But here. If there isn't so much as a case of mumps in——"

"Would it have to be mumps?" said his uncle. "Of course, if you're aching for mumps, I guess it could be arranged. But how many new souls do you suppose we get here a day?"

"Sizable lot, I expect."

"And how many of them get here in first-class condition?" said Uncle Frank triumphantly. "Why, I've seen Doctor Rush—Benjamin Rush—come back so tired from a day's round he could hardly flap one pinion against the other. Oh, if it's work you want—And then, of course, there's the earth."

"Hold on," said Doc Mellhorn. "I'm not going to appear

to any young intern in wings and a harp. Not at my time of life. And, anyway, he'd laugh himself sick."

"'Tain't that," said Uncle Frank. "Look here. You've left children and grandchildren behind you, haven't you? And they're going on?"

"Yes," said Doc Mellhorn.

"Same with what you did," said Uncle Frank. "I mean the inside part of it—that stays. I don't mean any funny business—voices in your ear and all that. But haven't you ever got clean tuckered out, and been able to draw on something you didn't know was there?"

"Pshaw, any man's done that," said Doc Mellhorn. "But you take the adrenal——"

"Take anything you like," said Uncle Frank placidly. "I'm not going to argue with you. Not my department. But you'll find it isn't all adrenalin. Like it here?" he said abruptly. "Feel satisfied?"

"Why, yes," said Doc Mellhorn surprisedly, "I do." He looked around the grape arbour and suddenly realised that he felt happy.

"No, they wouldn't all arrive in first-class shape," he said to himself. "So there'd be a place." He turned to Uncle Frank. "By the way," he said diffidently, "I mean, I got back so quick—there wouldn't be a chance of my visiting the other establishment now and then? Where I just came from? Smith and Ferguson are all right, but I'd like to keep in touch."

"Well," said Uncle Frank, "you can take that up with the delegation." He arranged the handkerchief in his breast pocket. "They ought to be along any minute now," he said. "Sister's been in a stew about it all day. She says there won't be enough chairs, but she always says that."

"Delegation?" said Doc Mellhorn. "But——"

"You don't realise," said Uncle Frank, with his rich chuckle. "You're a famous man. You've broken pretty near every regulation except the fire laws, and refused the Gate first crack. They've got to do something about it."

"But——" said Doc Mellhorn, looking wildly around for a place to escape.

"Sh-h!" hissed Uncle Frank. "Hold up your head and

look as though money were bid for you. It won't take long
—just a welcome." He shaded his eyes with his hand.
"My!" he said, with frank admiration, "you've certainly
brought them out. There's Rush, by the way."

"Where?" said Doc Mellhorn.

"Second from left, third row, in a wig," said Uncle
Frank. "And there's——"

Then he stopped, and stepped aside. A tall, grave figure
was advancing down the grape arbour—a bearded man with
a wise, majestic face who wore robes as if they belonged to
him, not as Doc Mellhorn had seen them worn in college
commencements. There was a small fillet of gold about his
head and in his left hand, Doc Mellhorn noticed without
astonishment, was a winged staff entwined with two fang-
less serpents. Behind him were many others. Doc Mellhorn
stood straighter.

The bearded figure stopped in front of Doc Mellhorn.
"Welcome, Brother," said Aesculapius.

"It's an honour to meet you, Doctor," said Doc Mellhorn. He shook the outstretched hand. Then he took a
silver half-dollar from the mouth of the left-hand snake.

I DON'T KNOW WHY EVERYBODY keeps on going to Angelo's. The drinks aren't any better—in fact, they're a little worse, if anything—and the dinner never was much. I'm getting so I can hardly look a sardine in the eye any more.

Of course it's a quiet place, and they don't let in many college boys. It's generally just the old crowd from five o'clock on. Oh, people come and go naturally—the way they do in New York. If they didn't, I don't suppose Angelo could keep on running. But what I mean is, you can drop in almost any time after curfew and find somebody you know to have a quick one or a couple of quick ones with. And then, if that's your weakness, you can stay and get dinner; though I wish they'd try another brand of sardines.

Suppose everyone stopped coming all at once? Or suppose the place closed? I don't like to think about that. I suppose its bound to happen, sooner or later, when Angelo's made his pile—they always go back to Iatly. Then there'll be all the trouble and bother of finding another place; and the crowd won't be the same. You can't keep a crowd together, once you move the place, in New York. It seems pretty safe, though, at the moment, I'm glad to say. There's never been any real trouble, you see; no one ever gets shot at Angelo's, and when the visiting firemen get too noisy, Rocco just eases them out. Rocco's the little one with the grin, and he doesn't look strong, but how he can ease a fellow out when it's necessary! He did it to me only once, and I've never held it against him. That was just after Evie and I had broken up.

No, I don't think there's any need to worry for a while yet. And when there is, I'm sure Angelo will tell me about it far enough ahead so I can make any arrangements. After all, I'm one of his oldest customers. I don't go back to the Twelfth Street place, the way Mr. Forman does, but seven years is a long time in this man's town. They're easing Mr. Forman out at 11.30 these days. It used to be all hours when I first knew him, but a man can't expect to drink like that at his age and not show it in the whites of the eyes. That's another thing I have against all this changing around. You get started going from one place to another and buying taxis and going in for general snake dancing; and before you know where you are you're on a party, and the whole next day is bad. Well, now, if you work at all, you can't afford to have the weekdays go bad on you. I'm not talking of Saturday night—there's a law about that. And, of course, those impromptu harvest homes are a lot of fun when you're young and new to the town. But when you've had a little sense knocked into you you're a fool if you don't run on schedule. Isn't that so?

Now, at Angelo's, you always know where you are. A couple of quick ones or so before dinner, and the red at dinner—or the white, if you're dining with a girl. Then a little touch after the coffee and a couple of long ones and a nightcap, and home at twelve by the old college clock. And all the time you're talking with somebody you know— about their wives, or their husbands, or religion, or the market, or what's new in the crowd—just rational conversation and maybe a little quiet singing, like "Work is the Curse of the Drinking Classes." Sometimes Mr. Forman sits down and tells one of his long stories, but generally he'd rather stand at the bar. And sometimes the whole crowd clicks, and sometimes it doesn't, and sometimes that Page girl gets started on her imitations.

But, anyway, it's something you're used to, and you're doing it again, and it's warm, and you know the people, and you don't have to go home. And Angelo's there, getting a little fatter and sleeker every year, and with a little bigger white edge around his waistcoat. Now and then he'll set up some *strega* for you, if he's feeling right. I don't like *strega* myself, but it would hurt his feelings to refuse. And then, in summer, there's the little back garden, and the fat cat that always has kittens, and the pink shades on the lamps. Rocco will be telling you the fish is ver' fine—and you know it isn't, but who cares?—and you can sit and watch the lights in the skyscrapers and hear the roar of the town, going by outside. You don't have to think at all. It's restful that way.

I can remember when I used to think a lot. And wonder about the people who came to places like Angelo's, and who they were, and why they came, and what they did with the rest of their time. I used to make up stories about them, going back to the apartment with Evie, and we'd both get excited over them; and forget to turn off at our own corner, we were talking so hard. That was when everybody we met was brand-new and bound to be interesting, and it was fun going to shows together in the gallery and having pancakes afterward at Childs'. I was always going to write some of those stories down, and she helped me make notes of them. I found the start of the one about Mr. Forman the other day. Well, what was the percentage in keeping it? I've seen a good deal of this writing racket since; and I ought to know what will sell and what won't. And, anyhow, I'd just made him an old soak, and he's really a pretty interesting man.

Besides, that's something you get over. Wondering, I mean. Once you're on a norml schedule, you don't have time. I used to think it was funny—meeting people the way you do and having them tell you all sorts of inside things, the way it happens, and yet not really knowing them or tying them up with anything outside. But that's stopped bothering me. You just have to let them come and go, or it breaks the charm.

Going home to dinner with Jim Hewitt was what cured me, finally. I never met a fellow I liked better at Angelo's, and we told our real names. So, when he suggested breaking the family bread one evening, I took him up. Good Lord, he lived at Scarsdale and they had three children! The baby was sounding off like a police siren as we came in, and we had one round of weak orange blossoms before the fodder. Mrs. Hewitt liked orange blossoms. Then, afterward, we sat around and played three-handed bridge and Mrs. Hewitt and Jim discussed the squeak in the car. I couldn't have stayed all night; I'd have had the mimies. Jim was sort of ritzy for a while after that, but he got all right again, finally. I guess they must have hitched up the sled-dogs and moved north to White Plains or something, for I haven't seen him for I don't know how long.

Of course, now and then something comes along that you have to take notice of. People get married or divorced, and Angelo will always open a bottle of champagne, no matter which it is, if they're really old customers. I remember the party the crowd of us gave to cheer up Helen Ashland when she heard about Jake's remarriage. She certainly took it like a sport—we were thinking up funny telegrams to send the bridal couple all evening. I don't believe she really had hysterics either. That was just Bing Otis' idea. And she couldn't have meant it when she said she hated us—she'd always been the life of the crowd. Anyhow, I think she got married again last year—somebody was broadcasting about it. If she ever comes back to Angelo's, I'll have to get the low-down.

That's another thing about the crowd—the way they stick together when anything happens. I'll never forget the night Ted Harrison went out. Of course, he'd been going into reverse for quite a while, and whenever he got particularly sunk, he'd talk about doing a one-way jump through a window; but we knew Ted and just kidded him along. So when he did do it, after all, it was mean. Anyhow, he had the sense not to stage his act at Angelo's.

We went to the service afterward—those of us that could. That's what I mean by all of us sticking together. It was one of those grey winter days, and cold. There was a little boy, and he was crying. I don't see why they brought him there. I didn't know Ted had a boy. I know the rest of Ted's family sort of upstaged us. But we felt we ought to be there; though it was funny how little you could remember about Ted except parties. Well, there isn't much to those services, the way I look at it. But then we went back to Angelo's and he was fine.

Evie never took to Angelo's somehow, even at first. She felt she had to like the dinner, because it was cheap, but the atmosphere of the place never really appealed to her. She liked going to places where there was music or where somebody famous might be sitting at the next table. Of course, it was generally an out-of-town buyer or a cloak model, really, but she got just as big a kick out of pretending. We used to have dinner home a lot, too, that first year.

81

It's wonderful how much food you can get for the money, living like that. Though, of course, it's really cheaper for me to eat at Angelo's, now I'm alone.

I've thought sometimes of getting a regular maid or one of those Japs who just come in and get dinner and clear away. There'd be money enough, for Evie never would take alimony, and now she's married again she doesn't need it, anyway. But then, what would you do after dinner? You can't go to the movies every night in the week, and a man who works all day needs some relaxation.

When Evie and I were married, we used to go to all sorts of places—we even went to museums on Sundays and to those concerts they have way up-town. But there's not much point in doing that sort of thing by yourself. And if you start trotting a girl around, why, anybody knows how that finishes. You may not mean to get hooked up together at all, but some little thing happens and you're in for it, one way or the other. And if it's one way, you're bound to feel like a bum sooner or later, while if it's the other—well, I've been married to Evie, and once is enough. I'm not going to repeat at my age. This child is too wise.

Now, you can see as much of a girl as you like at Angelo's, and that's all right because you're both part of the crowd. You've got protection, if you see what I mean. And even if you should stop playing for matches, it wouldn't mean much to either of you. We're all pretty modern in the crowd and we understand about things like that. Of course, we've had some fairly wild birds at one time or another, and I don't say I agree with all the talk I hear. But there's no use being Victorian, like people were in 1910. You just have to be wise.

It's queer, though—you certainly couldn't call Evie Victorian. And yet she never genuinely fitted in with the crowd. She wasn't a gloom either, or a blue-nose; she was really awfully pretty and the kind of girl that everybody likes right off. Why, Mr. Forman took a great shine to her and used to come over and sit at our table and tell her how he wished he had a daughter her age. But she just couldn't stand him. She said it was the look of his hands. Now, when anybody's been drinking for thirty semesters or so, like Mr.

Forman, I think they're lucky if they have any hands at all.
And if they do remind you of an alligator-skin bag, you
ought to overlook it and be broad-minded. But Evie simply
couldn't see it that way.

She was always wanting us to make friends with other
young married people, even when they lived up by Grant's
Tomb, where the climate's different. Well, that's all right,
but once you go in for that sort of thing, you might as well
stay in Waynesburg. That's what I kept telling her: "This
is New York," I said, "this is New York." Let the Weather
Bureau worry about the wide-open spaces. But all the same,
after she was gone, I found a whole envelope full of real-
estate ads—you know, those mortgage manors with the
built-in kiddie coops that all the Westchester cowboys
come home to on the 5.49. Now, can you imagine that in
a sensible girl?

So there it was, you see, and we didn't make a go of it.
Well, it's no use crying over spilt giggle-water, as they say,
and a man has to take things like that in his stride. If he
doesn't, he's lost in the shuffle in this man's hamlet. I can
see it wasn't anybody's fault; I'm modern. Maybe if Evie
had really liked the crowd—but there, I won't blame her.
She's happy the way she is, I guess; and you can see the
way I am. The only thing that ever hurts this little head is
to think of Angelo's closing down, sardines or no sardines.
But I'm sure he'll give me the eye, long enough ahead, if it
does. He's always shot square with me.

Of course, occasionally you get sort of philosophic about
this time in the evening, and wonder how things would
have turned out if they'd been different. But I've almost
quit doing that. There's no percentage in it.

I remember Mr. Forman, one of the first times Evie and
I were here. She hadn't noticed his hands then, and when
he got talking to us, we both thought he was a pretty quaint
old character. I guess he took to us so because we both of
us must have looked young and green. Anyhow, he started
philosophising. "Youth," he says. "Youth against the city;
coming in every day——" Oh, he ought to have had it
syndicated! "I've watched 'em come," says he, "and I've
seen 'em go. And some it makes, and some it breaks, and

some just dry up gradually till the whitewing sweeps 'em away. Go back to your cornfields, young people," says he— as if Waynesburg didn't have car-tracks!—"Go back and raise a family of nice little mortgages, because I'm a bad old man and you're breaking my heart"—and pretty soon he's crying into his glass.

We didn't pay any attention to him. We knew we were going to lick the world. But all the same, there's something in what he said. This town is a tough spot till you get wise to it—and it's too bad to see a fine man like Mr. Forman going to pieces the way he has these last two years. But then he's got what I call too much system in his drinking. You have to have just enough so it doesn't worry you.

Take me. If I'm stepping out a little more than usual to-night, it's just because of seeing Evie again. Of course, it was bound to happen some time, the way people come to New York; but a thing like that is apt to make you a little nervous just the same. It's easier, being modern the way we are. All the same, when I stepped out of the elevator and saw her waiting where she generally used to wait . . .

She hadn't come upstairs to the office, and that was decent of her. That girl at the front desk never could see me, and it's a laugh, your ex-wife ringing you up to pass the time of day or waiting out in the reception room. Though it wouldn't have been exactly a laugh to me.

I'd thought of all sorts of things to say to her when we did meet, but I didn't say any of them. I even forgot to take off my hat. I just said: "Hello, Evie. I didn't know you were in town," and she said: "Hello, Dick. I'm just here between trains"—and then we stared at each other.

I knew her right away, and yet I didn't know her, if you can get that. She was just as pretty as ever, but we weren't married any more. And then, her face was different. It didn't have that sort of quiet look on it when we were married. Of course, she'd let her hair grow too. She always had pretty hair. It had been five years. Well, there we were.

I must have looked like something, for, when we were out on the street she touched me on the arm.

"Don't worry, Dick," she said. "Everything's all right. I

just thought, as long as I was in New York, it was silly not to see each other. Do you mind?"

"Not a bit," I said. . . . Well, you have to be polite, haven't you?

"How's Mr. Barris?" I said. . . . That's Evie's husband. It's a funny name.

"Oh, he's fine . . ." she said, "just fine."

"And the children?" I said. . . . I couldn't imagine them. "I suppose they're fine too?"

"Oh, they're fine," she said.

"Well, I'm glad to hear that, Evie," I said.

I don't know why it was so hard to talk; we ought to have been used to talking to each other.

She looked at me and laughed, quite the way she used to. "We can't stand here and gape at each other, Dick," she said.

"That's right," I said, so I flagged a taxi and told him Angelo's. Then I remembered she didn't like Angelo's. But she was decent and said that it was all right.

I'll hand it to Rocco. He knew who she was, all right, but he didn't even bat an eye—just took the order. We were the only people in the little room. She said she wanted some sherry; so that was that, with a double old-fashioned for me.

When he was gone, "Was that Rocco?" she said. "He didn't remember me."

"Well," said I, "you've been away a long time."

Then we looked at each other and knew we had nothing to say. She made rings with the bottom of the sherry-glass.

"Oh, Dick," she said, "it's all so different from the way I thought it would be. Tell me about yourself."

"Oh, I'm still at the old stand," I said. "Same desk, as a matter of fact. Same salary, just about."

"How about the novel?"

"Oh," I said, "I'm working at it."

But she saw through me. "It's been five years," she said.

"A good idea's worth putting time on," said I, so she gave that up. Well, I wasn't going to cry on her.

"How about yourself?" said I. "Still living in Des Moines?"

STEPHEN VINCENT BENÉT

"You know Mr. Barris lives in Cleveland," she said.

"I never can keep those two towns straight," I said. I felt better now, with that old-fashioned inside me, especially as Rocco was bringing another.

"Who came from Waynesburg?" she said, trying to kid me out of it.

"Me," I said. "But you'll have to admit I've come a long way."

I don't know why that made her look as if she wanted to cry. She hardly ever did cry—that was one thing about her.

"Oh, show me the snapshots!" I said. "I know you've got them." So she did. There was the house and the children and everything, including Mr. Barris in golf pants, and the family sedan. The little girl looks like Evie. That's a break for her. I don't know what our kids would have looked like. Terrible, I suppose.

I passed the pictures back. "They're nice," I said. "It's quite a house. I suppose you've even got a garbage incinerator."

"Of course," she said. "Why?"

"It looks like a house that would have a bargage incinerator," I said. "But you'd think Barris could afford a better car now he's a family man."

"Don't talk about George," she said.

"I'm through," I said. "So you're happy, Evie?"

She looked straight at me. "I am happy," she said—and that's the hell of it; I could see she was.

"Well," I said, "skoal!"—and that was the end of that old-fashioned. I was certainly coming back to normal in grand style. I could feel it creeping all over me. Then I heard her sort of talking to herself.

"It was a mistake," she was saying. "I ought to have known, but I couldn't help it. I thought——"

"Why say that?" I said. "It's always nice to revive old times. . . . Rocco! . . . Ah, there you are, sir. And in a minute some of the crowd may blow in."

She started putting on her gloves. "I suppose they're the same too," she said.

"Who?"

86

"Oh, the Parsons, and that man you called the Poached Egg, and—what was her name?—Ruth something . . . . and——"

"Wait a minute," I said. "You're moving too fast for me. The Parsons broke up, and they say she's up at Saranac for her lungs. I don't know whatever did happen to the Poached Egg. As for that Ruth girl—well, after Ted Harrison popped himself——"

"Ted Harrison?" she said. "Who was Ted Harrison?"

Well, there we were. We just didn't have any point of contact at all. Of course, it wasn't her fault; she'd been away, and you do get quick action in this town. But she didn't even know who Ted Harrison had been.

"Oh, well," I said, "it doesn't signify. Just wait around a little. Some people I want you to meet will be coming in pretty soon. You'll like them; they're really awfully nice people."

"I don't think I can wait, Dick," she said. "I've got to get back to the hotel. I'm taking the night train."

"Back to Cleveland?" I said.

"Back to Cleveland," she said.

"Well," I said, "if you must, you must. And I won't tell Barris on you." I felt pretty cheery by now. She looked at me. "I'm sorry." I said.

"Oh, Dick, Dick!" she said. "Whatever are you going to do with your life? You had such a lot. I can't stand it."

"If you mean my hair," I said, "it's the barber's fault, not mine."

But she didn't pay any attention. "I didn't come back to show off," she said. "Really I didn't. I hoped—I really did—I'd come back and find you——"

"Clean and sober?" said I. "Well, I'm all of that."

"I—oh, what's the use?—I even thought you might be married."

"To some nice girl?" I said. "No, thanks. I've been."

"I held on as long as I could," she said.

"I'm not denying it," said I. "Let's leave it at that. No hard feelings."

She looked as if she wanted to say a whole lot more. Then she looked around the room and at Rocco coming in with the fresh supply. I don't know what she saw to make her look like that.

"No, it wouldn't have been," she said, sort of low to herself. "It couldn't have been. Good-bye, Dick, and thank you."

"The pleasure is all mine," said I. "Only sorry you won't have another. Just a second and I'll get you a taxi."

But when I'd settled the bill and got my hat and coat, she was gone.

I went back to the little room and sat down again. I didn't feel like thinking, but I couldn't help it. For one thing, Evie's asking about all those people who had been in the crowd—why, they'd just disappeared. And I hadn't even realised it. Come to think of it, the only two left of that particular crowd who still came to Angelo's were Mr. Forman and myself. And what was that novel about that I'd been going to write?

"Rocco!" I called.

"Right with you, mister."

"You have the right idea," I said, but when he came in, I made him stay.

"Rocco," I said, "tell me something. How do I look to-day?"

"Oh, mister look ver' fine; seem ver' well."

That's the trouble with Rocco. He's always so darn pleasant.

"Don't two-time me, Rocco," I said. "Do you remember when I first started coming here?"

"Oh, yes; remember ver' well. Mister ver' good customer; ver' steady customer. Wish we had all like mister."

"Leave that outside," I said. "Just tell me one thing: Do I look a lot different?"

He spread out his hands. "Sure, mister look little different. Why not? Time pass. Rocco look different too."

"You're a liar," I said. "You haven't changed that Dago grin in twenty years. . . . All right, I look different, but how old do I look?"

He spread out his hands again. "Rocco don't know. Mister maybe forty, forty-one—mister in his prime."

"You low snake," I said. "I'm thirty-two." This was serious.

"Thirty-two? That's right. That's what Rocco mean"— and he grinned. But I didn't feel so funny.

"Tell me, Rocco," I said. "You've always been a friend of mine. Now be a friend. Tell me honestly. Do you think I drink too much?"

Gosh, you couldn't get anywhere with him. He just kept on grinning.

"Mister ver' good customer," he said; "ver' old, ver' steady customer. Mister carry what he drink ver' well."

"I know that!" I said. I was getting mad by now. "But is it too much? Be sensible, Rocco. I don't put away half what Mr. Forman does."

"Nobody drink so much as Mr. Forman. Some day Mr. Forman go pop. Rocco ver' sorry then, for Mr. Forman old customer."

"Well, that's a swell way of encouraging me. How about yourself, Rocco? How's your health?"

"Fine, thanks, mister. We have new bambino only other day."

"Well, I'm certainly glad to hear that. But look here, Rocco; you take a snifter——"

"Sure. Rocco drink wine—*strega*—ver' good. But Rocco have to work. Can't drink alla time."

"I get that. But I work too."

"Sure, mister work. But Rocco work alla time. Rocco have wife, tree bambini; have to work. Work to go back to Italy, buy *trattoria*, buy farm, have more bambini, be big man in town. That work for a man. Mister have another old-fashioned?"

He wouldn't talk any more. And the next one didn't go so well, because I'd started looking at myself in the mirror.

Oh, it just shows what a state I was in. And it shows you never ought to go back on your tracks. You know, for a while there I didn't like my face a bit.

That's why I say, modern or not, things like seeing Evie again don't do you any good. Because, when Mr. Forman came in and touched me on the shoulder, I jumped a mile. And just before I jumped I caught his face in the glass right over mine. I've apologised to him since, and I guess he's forgotten it. But they all must have thought I was crazy, running out like that and leaving the money on the table. And all that week I just got crazier and crazier, getting up and taking a cold shower in the mornings, and eating at tea-rooms and coming right back after dinner and hunting around to see if I could find whatever became of that novel. One good thing, I did get the room pretty well cleaned up. That woman who comes in never really cleans.

But what's the use of all that when you keep getting the fidgets? And getting the fidgets makes you think too much. Anyway, one evening it was nice and warm, and I thought, "I'll just take a walk. I can't sit here any more."

Well, I didn't have any particular direction in mind, but after a while, sure enough, there I was in front of Angelo's. Man, you should have seen the welcome they gave me. Angelo set up the drinks himself, and Rocco was grinning all over.

"Angelo think we lose our mos' steady customer," he said, "but mister come back. I know he come back."

And Mr. Forman never said a word about how I'd acted.

He wasn't a bit stand-offish; in fact, Rocco had to ease him out at eleven that night.

Now, the only worry I've got is Angelo's retiring, as I say. But even if he does, maybe Rocco will keep the place on. Of course, even that would be a change, but I'd hardly mind. We've known each other a long while, and he knows I'm a good customer.

THE LAST OF THE LEGIONS

THE GOVERNOR WANTED to have everything go off as quietly as possible, but he couldn't keep the people from the windows or off the streets. After all, the legion had been at Deva ever since there was a town to speak of, and now we were going away. I don't want to say anything against the Sixth or the Second—there are good men under all the eagles. But we're not called the Valeria Victrix for nothing, and we've had the name some few centuries. It takes a legion with men in it to hold the north-west.

I think, at first, they intended to keep the news secret, but how could you do that, in a town? There's always someone who tells his girl in strict confidence, and then there are all the peddlers and astrologers and riff-raff, and the sharp-faced boys with tips on the races or the games. I tell you, they knew about it as soon as the general or the governor—not to speak of the rumours before. As a matter of fact, there had been so many rumours that, when the orders came at last, it was rather a relief. You get tired of telling women that nothing will happen to them even if the legion does go, and being stopped five times in ten minutes whenever you go into town.

All the same, I had to sit up half the night with one recruit of ours. He had a girl in the town he was mad about, and a crazy notion of deserting. I had to point out to the young imbecile that even if the legion goes, Rome stays, and describe the two men I'd happened to see flogged to death, before he changed his mind. The girl was a pretty little weak-mouthed thing—she was crying in the crowd when we marched by, and he bit his lips to keep steady. But I couldn't have him deserting out of our cohort—we haven't had a thing like that happen in twenty years.

It was queer, their not making more noise. They tried to cheer—governor's orders—when we turned the camp over to the native auxiliaries in the morning, but it wasn't much of a success. And yet, the auxiliaries looked well enough, for auxiliaries. I wouldn't give two cohorts of Egyptians for them myself, but they had their breastplates shined and kept a fairly straight front. I imagined they'd dirty up our quarters—auxiliaries always do—and that wasn't pleasant to think of. But the next legion that came to Deva—us or another—would put things straight again. And it couldn't be long.

Then we had our own march past—through the town—and, as I say, it was queer. I'm a child of the camp—I was brought up in the legion. The tale is that the first of us came with Cæsar—I don't put much stock in that—and of course we've married British ever since. Still, I know what I know, and I know what a crowd sounds like, on most occasions. There's the mutter of a hostile one, and the shouts when they throw flowers, and the sharp, fierce cheering when they know you're going out to fight for them. But this was different. There wasn't any heart or pith in it —just a queer sort of sobbing wail that went with us all the way to the gates. Oh, here and there, people shouted: "Come back with their heads!" or, "Bring us a Goth for a pet!" the way they do, but not as if they believed what they were saying. Too many of them were silent, and that queer sort of sobbing wail went with us all the way.

I marched with the first cohort; it wasn't so bad for me. Though here and there, I saw faces in the crowd—old Elfrida, who kept the wine shop, with the tears running down her fat cheeks, shouting like a good one, and Parmesius, the usurer, biting his nails and not saying anything at all. He might have given us a cheer; he'd had enough of our money. But he stood there, looking scared. I expect he was thinking of his money-bags and wondering if somebody would slip a knife in his ribs at night. We'd kept good order in the town.

It took a long time, at the gates, for the governor had to make a speech—like all that old British stock, he tries to be more Roman than the Romans. Our general listened to him, sitting his horse like a bear. He's a new general, one of Stilicho's men, and a good one in spite of his hairiness and his Vandal accent. I don't think he cared very much for the governor's speech—it was the usual one. The glorious Twentieth, you know, and our gallant deeds, and how glad they'd be to have us back again. Well, we knew that without his telling—we could read it in the white faces along the walls. They were very still, but you could feel them, looking. The whole town must have been at the walls. Then the speech ended, and our general nodded his bear head and we marched. I don't know how long they stayed at the walls—I couldn't look back.

But my recruit got away, after all, at the second halt, and that bothered me. He was a likely-looking young fellow, though I'd always thought his neck was too long. Still, he was one of the children of the camp—you wouldn't have picked him to desert. After that, half a dozen others tried it—those things are like a disease—but our general caught two and made an example, and that stopped the rest. I don't care for torture, myself—it leaves a bad taste in your mouth—but there are times when you have to use a firm hand. They were talking too much about Deva and remembering too many things. Well, I could see, myself, that if we had to be marched half across Britain to take ship at Anderida, that meant the Northmen were strong again. And I wouldn't like to hold the north-west against Northmen and Scots with nothing but auxiliaries. But that was the empire's business—it wasn't mine.

After it was over, I was having a cup of wine and chatting with Agathocles—he's a small man, but clever with the legion accounts and very proud that his father was a Greek. He has special privileges and that's apt to get a man disliked, but I always got along well with him. If you're senior centurion, you have your own rights, and he didn't often try the nasty side of his tongue on me.

"Well, Death's-Head," I said—we call him that because of his bony face—"were you present at the ceremonies?"

"Oh, I was present," he said. He shivered a little. "I suppose you liked hearing them squeal," he said, with his black eyes full of malice.

"Can't say that I did," I said, "but it'll keep the recruits in order."

"For a while," he said, and laughed softly. But I wasn't really thinking of the men who had been caught—I was thinking of my own recruit who'd got away. I could see him, you know, quite plainly, with his long neck and his bright blue Northern eyes—a tiny, running figure, hiding in ditches and travelling by night. He'd started in full marching order, too, like an idiot. Pretty soon, he'd be throwing pieces of equipment away. And what would he do when he did get back to Deva—hide on one of the outlying farms? Our farmers were a rough lot—they'd turn him over to the governor, if they didn't cut his throat for the price of his armour. It's a bad feeling, being hunted—I've had it myself. You begin to hear noises in the bracken and feel the joints in your armour where an arrow could go through. He'd scream, too, if he were caught—scream like a hare. And all for a weak-faced girl and because he felt homesick! I couldn't understand it.

"Worried about your recruit?" said Agathocles, though I hadn't said a word.

"The young fool!" I said. "He should have known better."

"Perhaps he was wiser than you think," said Agathocles. "Perhaps he's a soothsayer and reads omens."

"Soothsayer!" I said. "He'll make a pretty-looking soothsayer if the governor catches him! Though I suppose he has friends in the town."

"Why, doubtless," said Agathocles. "And, after all, why should they waste a trained man? He might even change his name and join the auxiliaries. He might have a good story, you know."

I thought, for a moment. Of course they'd be slack, now we'd left, but I couldn't believe they'd be as slack as that.

"I should hope not, I'm sure," I said, rather stiffly. "After all, the man's a deserter."

"Old Faithful," said Agathocles, laughing softly. "Always Old Faithful. You like the boy, but you'd rather see him cut to ribbons like our friends to-day. Now, I'm a Greek and a philosopher—I look for causes and effects."

"All Greeks are eaters of wind," I said, not insultingly, you know, but just to show him where he stood. But he didn't seem to hear me.

"Yes," he said, "I look for causes and effects. You think

the man a deserter, I think him a soothsayer—that is the difference between us. Would a child of the camp have deserted the legion a century ago, or two centuries ago, Old Faithful?"

"How can I tell what anyone would do a century ago?" I said, for it was a foolish question.

"Exactly," he said. "And a century ago they would not have withdrawn the Twentieth—not from that border—not unless Rome fell." He clapped me on the back with an odious familiarity. "Do not worry about your recruit, Old Faithful," he said. "Perhaps he will even go over to the other side, and, indeed, that might be wise of him."

"Talk treason to your accounts, Greek," I growled, "and take your hand off my shoulder. I am a Roman."

He looked at me with sad eyes.

"After three hundred years in Britain," he said. "And yet he says he is a Roman. Yes, it is a very strong law. And yet we had a law and states once, too, we Greeks. Be comforted, my British Roman. I am not talking treason. After all, I, too, have spent my life with the eagles. But I look for causes and effects."

He sighed in his wine-cup and, in spite of his nonsense, I could not help but feel sorry for him. He was not a healthy man and his chest troubled him at night.

"Forget them," I said, "and attend to your accounts. You'll feel better when we're really on the march."

He sighed again. "Unfortunately, I am a philosopher," he said. "It takes more than exercise to cure that. I can even hear a world cracking, when it is under my nose. But you are not a philosopher, Old Faithful—do not let it give you bad dreams."

I manage to get my sleep without dreams, as a rule, so I told him that and left him. But, all the same, some of his nonsense must have stuck in my head. For, all the way down to Anderida, I kept noticing little things. Usually, on a long march, once you get into the swing of it, you live in that swing. There's the back of the neck of the man in front of you, and the weather, fine or wet, and the hairy general, riding his horse like a bear, and the dust kicked up by the column and the business of billets for the night. The

town life drops away from you like the cloak you left behind in the pawnshop and, pretty soon, you've never led
any other kind of life. You have to take care of your men
and see the cooks are up to their work and tell from the look
on a man's face whether he's the sort of fool who rubs his
feet raw before he complains. And all that's pleasant enough
and so is the change in the country, and the villages you
go through, likely never to see again, but there was good
wine in one, and a landlord's daughter in another, and perhaps you washed your feet in a third and joked with the
old girl who came down by the stream and told you you
were a fine-looking soldier. It's all there, and nothing to
remember, but pleasant while it lasts. And, toward the end,
there's the little tightness at the back of the mind that makes
you know you're coming near the fighting. But, before
that, you hardly think at all.

This wasn't any different and yet I kept looking at the
country. I'd been south before, as far as Londinium, but
not for years, and there's no denying that it's a pleasant
land. A little soft, as the people are, but very green, very
smiling, between the forests. You could see they took
care of their fields; you could see it was a rich place, com-
pared to the north. There were sheep in the pastures,
whole flocks of them, fat and baa-ing, and the baths in the
towns we passed through got better all the way. And yet I
kept looking for places where a cohort or two could make a
stand without being cut off completely—now, why should
I do that? You can say it was my business, but Mid-Britain
has been safe for years. You have only to look at the villas—
we've got nothing like them in the north-west. I couldn't
help wondering what a crew of wild Scots or long-haired
Northmen would do to some of them. We'd have blocked
up half those windows where I come from—once they
start shooting fire arrows, big windows are a nuisance, even
in a fortified town.

And yet, in spite of the way Agathocles rode along like
a death's-head, it was reassuring too. For it showed you
how solid the empire was, a big solid block of empire,
green and smiling, with its magistrates and fine special
ladies and theatres and country houses, all the way from

Mid-Britain to Rome, and getting richer all the way. I didn't feel jealous about it or particularly proud, but there it was, and it meant civilised things. That's the difference between us and the barbarians—you may not think of it often, but, when you see it, you know. I remember a young boy, oh, eight or nine. He'd been sent down from the big house on his fat pony with his tutor, to look at the soldiers, and there he sat, perfectly safe, while his pony cropped the grass and the old man had a hand in the pony's mane. He was clean out of bowshot of the big house, and the hedges could have held a hundred men, but you could see he'd never been afraid in his life, or lived in disputed ground. Not even the old tutor was afraid—he must have been a slave, but he grinned at us like anything. Well, that shows you. I thought the worse of Agathocles, after that.

And yet, there were other things—oh, normal enough. But, naturally, you can't move a legion without people asking questions, and civilians are like hens when they start to panic. Well, we knew there was trouble in Gaul—that was all we could say. Still, they'd follow you out of the town, and that would be unpleasant. But that didn't impress me nearly as much as the one old man.

We'd halted for half an hour and he came down from his fields, a countryman and a farmer. He had a speckled straw hat on, but it takes more than a dozen years' farming to get the look out of a man's back.

"The Twentieth," he said slowly, when he saw our badge of the boar, "the Valeria Victrix. Welcome, comrade!" so I knew at once that he'd served. I gave him the regulation salute and asked him a question, and his eyes glowed.

"Marcus Hostus," he said. "Centurion of the Third Cohort of the Second, twenty years ago." He pulled his tunic aside to show me the seamed scar.

"That was fighting the Welsh tribesmen," he said. "They were good fighters. After that, they gave me my land. But I still remember the taste of black beans in a helmet," and he laughed a high old man's laugh.

"Well," I said, "I wouldn't regret them. You've got a nice little place here." For he had.

He looked around at his fields. The woman had come to

97

the door of the hut by then, with a half-grown girl beside her, and a couple of recruits were asking her for water.

"Yes," he said, "it's a nice little place and my sons are strong. There are two of them in the upper field. Are you halting for long, Centurion? I should like them to see the eagles before I die."

"Not for long," I said. "As a matter of fact, we're on our way to the sea-coast. They seem to need us in Gaul."

"Oh," he said, "they need you in Gaul. But you'll be coming back."

"As Cæsar wills it," I said. "You know what orders are, Centurion."

He looked at the eagles again.

"Yes," he said. "I know what orders are. The Valeria Victrix, the bulwark of the north-west. And you are marching to the ships—Oh, do not look at me, Centurion—I have been a centurion too. It must be a very great war that calls the Valeria Victrix from Britain."

"We have heard of such a war," I said, for he, too, had served with the eagles.

He nodded his old head once or twice. "Yes," he said, "a very great war. Even greater than the wars of Theodosius, for he did not take the Twentieth. Well, I can still use a sword."

I wanted to tell him that he would not have to use one, for there was the hut and the fields and the half-grown girl. But, looking at him, the words stuck in my throat. He nodded again.

"When the eagles go, Britain falls," he said, very quietly. "If I were twenty years younger, I would go back to the Second—that would be good fighting. Or, perhaps, to the Sixth, at Eboracum—they will not withdraw the Sixth till the last of all. As it is, I die here, with my sons." He straightened himself. "Hail, Centurion of the Valeria Victrix—and farewell," he said.

"Hail, Marcus Hostus, Centurion," I said, and they raised the eagles. I know that he watched us out of sight; though, again, I could not look back. It is true that he was an old man, and old men dream, but I was as glad that Agathocles had not heard his words.

For it seemed to me that Agathocles was always at my elbow and I grew very weary indeed of his company and his cough and what he called his philosophy. The march had done him no good—he was bonier than ever and his cheeks burned—but that did not stop his talkativeness. He was always pointing out to me little things I would hardly have noticed by myself—where a ploughland had been left fallow or where a house or a barn still showed the scars of old burnings. By Hercules! As if a man couldn't plant wheat for a year without the empire's falling—but he'd point and nod his head. And then he'd keep talking—oh, about the states and the law they'd had in Greece, long before the city was founded. Well, I never argue with a man about the deeds of his ancestors—it only makes bad feeling. But I told him once, to shut him up, that I knew about Athens. A friend of mine had been stationed there once and said they had quite decent games for a provincial capital. His eyes flashed at that and he muttered something in his own tongue.

"Yes," he said. "They have decent games there. And buildings that make the sacred Forum at Rome—which I have seen, by the way, and which you have not seen—look like a child's playing with mud and rubble. That was when we had states and a law. Then we fought with each other, and it went—yes, even before the man from Macedon. And then you came and now, at last, it is your turn. Am I sorry or glad? I do not know. Sorry, I think, for the life is out of my people—they are clever and will always be clever, but the life is out of them. And I am not philosopher enough not to grieve when an end comes."

"Oh, talk as you like, Agathocles," I said, for I was resolved he shouldn't anger me again. "But you'd better not talk like that in front of the general."

"Thank you, Old Faithful," he said, and coughed till he nearly fell from his mule. "But I do not talk like that to the general—only to persons of rare intelligence, like yourself. The general does not like me very well, as it is, but I am still useful with the accounts. Perhaps, when we get to Gaul—if we go to Gaul—he will have me flayed or impaled. I believe those are Vandal customs. Yes, that is very probable, I think, if my cough does not kill me before. But, meanwhile, I must observe—we Greeks are so curious."

"Observe all you like," I said, "but the legion's shaking down very nicely, it seems to me."

"Yes, shaking down very nicely," he said. "Do you ever think of your deserter, who went back to Deva? No, I thought not. And yet he was the first effect of the cause I seek, and there have been others since." He chuckled quite cheerfully at that and went along reciting Greek poetry to himself till the cough took him again. The poetry was all about the fall of a city called Troy—he translated some of it to me, and it sounded quite well, if you care for that sort of thing, though, as I pointed out to him, our own Vergil had covered the same subjects, as I understand it.

We had turned toward the sea-coast by then—we weren't going through Londinium after all. That disappointed our recruits, but of course the general was right about it. We'd kept excellent discipline so far, but it's a very different thing, letting men loose in a capital. I was sorry not to see it again myself. I told the men that when they complained. This was southern country we passed through, very soft and gentle; though, on the coasts, there is danger. But, when we halted for the night, there had been no danger for years—it was a wide pocket of peace.

I remember the look of the big painted rooms of the villa, when I was summoned there. A very fine villa it was —it belonged to a rich man. They'd had Roman names so long, they'd forgotten their own stock, though the master looked British enough when you looked him full in the face. They had winged cupids painted on the walls of the dining-room—they were sharpening arrows and driving little cars with doves—very pretty and bright. It must have been imported work—no Briton could paint like that. And the court-yard had orange-trees in it, growing in tubs—I know what an orange tree costs, for my cousin was a gardener. A swarm of servants, too, better trained than our northern ones and sneakingly insolent, as rich men's servants are apt to be. But they were all honey to me, and sticky speeches—they knew better than to mock an officer on duty.

Well, I went into the room, and there was my general and the master of the house, both with wreaths round their heads in the old-fashioned way, and Agathocles making notes on his tablets in a corner and hiding his cough with his hand. My general had his wreath on crooked and he looked like a baited bear, though they must have had a good feed, and he liked wine. There were other people in the room—some sons and sons-in-law—all very well dressed, but a little shrill in their conversation, as that sort is apt to be, but the master of the house and my general were the ones I noticed.

My general called me in and told them who I was, while I stood at attention and Agathocles coughed. Then he said: "This is my senior centurion. . . . And how many leagues does the legion cover in a day, Centurion?"

I told him, though he knew well enough.

"Good," he said, in his thick Vandal accent. "And how many leagues would we cover in a day—let me see—accompanied by civilians, with litters and baggage?"

I told him; though, of course, he knew. It was less, of course; it made a decided difference. A legion does not march like the wind—that is not its business—but civilians slow everything up. Especially when there are women.

"As I thought," he said to the master of the villa. "As you see, it is quite impossible," and, in spite of his crooked wreath, his eyes were bleak and shrewd. Then arose a babble of talk and expostulation from the sons and the sons-in-law. I have heard such talk before—it is always the same. As I say, rich men are apt to think that all government, including the army, exists for their personal convenience. I stood at attention, waiting to be dismissed.

The master of the villa waited till the others had had their say. He was a strong man with a beaky nose, much stronger than his sons. He waited till the babble had ceased, his eyes calm, regarding our general. Then he said, in the smooth, careless voice of such men:

"The general forgets, perhaps, that I am a cousin of the legate. I merely ask protection for myself and my house-

101

hold. And we would be ready to move—well, within twenty-four hours. Yes, I can promise you, within twenty-four hours." There was such perfect assurance in his voice that I could have admired the man.

"I am sorry not to oblige a cousin of the legate," said my general, with his bear's eyes gleaming dully. "Unfortunately, I have my orders."

"And yet," said the master of the villa, charmingly, "a certain laxity—a certain interpretation, let us say . . ."

He left his words in the air—you could see he had done this sort of thing before, and always successfully. You could see that, all his life, he had been accustomed to rules being broken for him because of his place and name. I have liked other generals better than this general—after all, the Vandals are different from us—but I liked the way he shook his head now.

"I have my orders," he said, and lay hunched like a bear on his couch.

"Let us hope you will never regret your strict interpretation of them, General," the master of the villa said without rancour, and a cool wind blew through the room. I felt the cool wind on my own cheek, though I am a senior centurion and my appeal is to Cæsar. The man was strong enough for that.

"Let us hope not," said my general gruffly, and rose. "Your hospitality has been very enjoyable." I must say, for a Vandal, he made his manners well. On the way out, the master of the villa stopped me unobtrusively.

"And what would it be worth, Centurion," he said in a low voice, "to carry a single man on your rolls who was not on your rolls before? A single man—I do not ask for more."

"It would be worth my head," I said; for though my general did not seem to be looking at me, I knew that he was looking.

The master of the villa nodded, and a curious, dazed look came over his strong face. "I thought so," he said, as if to himself. "And, after all, what then? My nephew in Gaul writes me that Gaul is not safe; my bankers in Rome write me that Rome itself is not safe. Will you tell me what place

102

is safe if Rome is not safe any more?" he said in a stronger voice, and caught at my arm. I did not know how to answer him, so I kept silent. He looked, suddenly, very much older than he had when I entered the room.

"A king's ransom out at loan and the interest of the interest," he muttered. "And yet, how is a man to be safe? And my cousin is the legate, too—I have first-hand information. They will not bring back the legions—blood does not flow back, once it is spilt. And yet, how can I leave my house here, with everything so uncertain?"

It seemed a fine house to me, though not very defensible; but, even as he spoke, I could see the rain beating through the walls. I could see the walls fallen, and the naked people, the barbarians, huddled around a dim fire. I had not believed that possible before, but now I believed it. There was ruin in the face of that man. I could feel Agathocles tugging at my elbow and I went away—out through the court-yard where the orange-trees stood in their tubs, and the bright fish played in the pool.

When we were back in our billets, Agathocles spoke to me.

"The general is pleased with you," he said. "He saw that they tried to bribe you, but you were not bribed. If you had been bribed, he would have had your head."

"Do I care for that?" I said, a little wildly. "What matters one head or another? But if Rome falls, something ends."

He nodded soberly, without coughing. "It is true," he said. "You had nothing but an arch, a road, an army and a law. And yet a man might walk from the east to the west because of it—yes, and speak the same tongue all the way. I do not admire you, but you were a great people."

"But tell me," I said, "why does it end?"

He shook his head. "I do not know," he said. "Men build and they go on building. And then the dream is shaken—it is shaken to bits by the storm. Afterwards, there follow darkness and the howling peoples. I think that will be for a long time. I meant to be a historian, when I first joined the eagles. I meant to write of the later wars of Rome as Thucydides wrote of the Greek wars. But now my ink is dry and I have nothing to say."

"But," I said, "it is there—it is solid—it will last," for I thought of the country we had marched through, and the boy, unafraid, on his pony.

"Oh," said Agathocles, "it takes time for the night to fall—that is what people forget. Yes, even the master of your villa may die in peace. But there are still the two spirits in man—the spirit of building and the spirit of destruction. And when the second drives the faster horse, then the night comes on."

"You said you had a state and a law," I said. "Could you not have kept them?"

"Why, we could," said Agathocles, "but we did not. We had Pericles, but we shamed him. And now you and I—both Romans"—and he laughed and coughed—"we follow a hairy general to an unknown battle. And, beyond that, there is nothing."

"They say it is Alaric, the Goth," I said. "They say he marches on Rome," for, till then, except in jest, we had not spoken of these wars.

"Alaric, or another, what matters?" said Agathocles, "Who was that western chieftain—he called himself Niall of the Hundred Battles, did he not? And we put him down, in the end, but there were more behind him. Always more. It is time itself we fight, and no man wins against time. How long has the legion been in Britain, Centurion?"

"Three hundred and fifty years and eight," I said, for that is something that even children know.

"Yes," said Agathocles, "the Valeria Victrix. And who remembers the legions that were lost in Parthia and Germany? Who remembers their names?"

But by then I had come back to myself and did not wish to talk to him.

"All Greeks are eaters of wind," I said. "Caw like a crow, if you like; I do not listen."

"It does not matter to me," he said, with a shrug, and a cough. "I tell you, I shall be flayed before the ending, unless my cough ends it. No sensible general would let me live, after the notes I have taken to-night. But have it your own way."

I did not mean to let him see that he had shaken me, but

he had. And when six days later, we came to Anderida and the sea, I was shaken again. The ships should have been ready for us, but they were not, though our general raged like a bear, and we had to wait four days at Anderida. That was hard, for in four days you get to know the look of a town. They had felt the strength of the sea pirates; they were not like Mid-Britain. I thought of my man at the villa and how he might die in peace, even as Agathocles had said. But all the time, the moss would be creeping on the stone and the rain beating at the door. Till, finally, the naked people gathered there, without knowledge—they would have forgotten the use of the furnace that kept the house warm in winter and the baths that made men clean. And the fields of my veteran centurion of the Second, would go back to witch-grass and cockleburs because they were too busy with killing to plant the wheat in the field. I even thought back to my deserter and saw him living, on one side or the other, but with memory of order and law and civilised things. Then that, too, would go, and his children would not remember it, except as a tale. I wanted to ask Agathocles what a race should leave to its kind, but I did not, for I knew he would talk of Greece, and I am a Roman.

Then we sailed, on a very clear day, with little wind, but enough to get us out of harbour. It came suddenly, as those things do, and we did not have time to think. I was very busy—it was only when we were ready to embark that I thought at all. I am a child of the camp and the legion is my hearth. But I knew, as we stood there, waiting, what we were leaving—the whole green, rainy, smoky, windy island, with its seas on either hand and its deep graves in the earth. We had been there three hundred and fifty and eight—we had been the Valeria Victrix. Now we followed a hairy general to an unknown battle, over the rim of the world, and we would win fights and lose them, but our time was over.

I heard the speech for the last time—the British Latin. After that, it would only be the legion, wherever we went. Our general stood like a bear—he would take care of us as long as he could. Agathocles looked seasick already—his face was pinched and thin, and he coughed behind his hand. Before us lay the wide channel and the great dark-ness. And the Sixth still held Eboracum—I wished, for a moment, that I had been with the Sixth.

"Get your packs on board, you sons!" I shouted to the men.

As the crowd began to cheer a little, I wanted to say to somebody: "Remember the Valeria Victrix! Remember our name!" But I could not have said it to anyone, and there was no time for those things.

THE BRIG WAS ALREADY a white-sailed toy on blue waters. Soon enough she would be hull down on the horizon, then nothing at all. No man among her crew would ever set foot again willingly on the island where that crew had marooned its captain. And Vasco Gomez, lost and alone on a pin-point of earth set down among waves that seemed to come from the other end of the world, stretched out his arms and laughed loudly for the first time since they had set him ashore.

He was known as a clever man and a lucky captain in every waterside tavern where the freebooters gathered. But this marooning of himself on a lost and uncharted island was the cleverest and luckiest exploit in a career that had held little mercy and no noteworthy failures.

It had not been an easy task. No, even for Vasco Gomez, it had not been easy. His own name for good fortune had worked against him, as had the quite justifiable fear his reputation inspired in the most hard-bitten of free companions. It had taken untiring craft and skill to bring even a crew of wolves to the *point* of mutiny against Vasco Gomez. And even greater art to see to it that these wolves, once roused, should maroon a living man where he wished to be, and not merely cast a hacked body overside.

But it had been done, and well done—his luck had held. He was alive—he was here. He had taken the first huge step toward his kingdom. And it was time, for, though he was still as strong in body as any three men of the crew that had deserted him, he knew by certain warnings that he had entered middle age.

Middle age. The drying up of the life in a man, the gradual slowing of the heart. And yet, a man stronger and more cunning than the run of men might still manage to have his cake and eat it too—to get off scot-free and whistling—even to grow old. A man like him, for example.

And more than scot-free—rich—if he knew a secret.

Rich. His eyes gleamed as he rolled the word on his tongue. He stared around him, measuring the extent of his riches.

They had left him without fresh water, but not a hundred paces inland was a spring and a stream. They had left him without victual, but he knew this island of old. There was provision for the crew of a frigate on the island; the unceasing provision of nature.

They had left him without tools or weapons, except for the sheath-knife hidden in his boot. But he had flint and steel, and the axes in the second cache should not have rusted by now, for they lay in dry soil. For that matter, if worst came to worst, he could hollow a boat by burning out a tree-bole. It might take time—but what was time to him, now? There was no time in this solitude—the measurements of time had ceased. There was only one long hour, his hour, the hour of his kingdom. He left the first wave of it wash over him, peacefully, slowly. His heart rose in his body to meet it, his lips drank it in.

"A long time on the way—you've been a long time on the way here, Vasco Gomez," he thought to himself. But it was over now. Pedro's treasure lay buried where it had always lain, not ten feet down, between the rock and the palm. He had not yet seen it with his eyes, but he knew that it was still there. For seven years he had carried the secret, locked under his ribs, closer to him than his heart.

He exhaled a long breath, staring back through the years. He was the only man alive who knew.

There had been others who had an inkling. He had made it his business to find them and see that they got no farther. There was a legend still, but a legend that few believed. And for a while, of course, there had been Pedro.

He saw the dark cruelty of that insatiable face swim up at him, in memory, like something seen through a wraith of sea fog. He smiled. Pedro was long since turned into leather at Execution Dock. He had not been able to come back, though he'd tried. But Vasco Gomez had come back. And, from the moment that he had landed on the island this noon, the treasure had been Pedro's no longer, but his treasure— the treasure of Vasco Gomez.

The men who had actually buried the spoil were safe

enough. Their bones lay in the second cache with the tools of their labour. They would not disturb him. The one thing that did disturb him was the thought that the bags and chests that held the treasure might have rotted. In that case he would have to make new ones, somehow—one could not put to sea with half a boat-load of naked gold.

Half a boat-load at the least; there might be more. It would be interesting to see the full extent of the loot. He had only caught hasty glimpses of it by the bad light of the lanterns, on that night that was burned in his memory. But there would be enough for his wants—enough at the least to buy fat days and fine feathers—or even God's pardon, perhaps, weighed out in masses and candles. Enough to buy love and hate—and age for Gomez.

And all that remained to be done was so simple. A week, two, to lift the treasure. Two months, three months, to make a boat and provision it. Longer, perhaps, for he would not attempt the sea journey in the stormy season, but what was time, now he had all time to spend? Then a sixty-mile sail in an open boat to that other island, a daring exploit for landsmen, but child's play for Vasco Gomez. There were tamed Indians on that other island; he knew them, he had been careful to make them his friends. Then a little policy —a little murder, perhaps—another ship—a little intrigue with the mainland—he knew the fellow who had the Governor's ear and how to use him. And after that, anything: a king's coat to wear, a king's commission to carry— "Our well-beloved Vasco Gomez"—a decent estate at home, a little respectability, a little repentance, an altar of rose marble in an old cathedral to hold God strictly to the bargain—and not only this world but the next one flung open for the penitent buccaneer.

All for gold—all there to be bought by gold. Nothing existed that could not be bought by gold.

He came out of his muse and stared seaward again, eagerly. The brig was only a speck, now; soon the abrupt night would come down. He must gather wood, make a fire, knock over a crab or two, find water, devise a bed. To-morrow he would start building a hut for himself. Perhaps he might even finish his boat before he lifted the treasure.

109

The treasure could wait—it would not run away. There was no time on earth that could take him from his treasure now.

It was one morning, when Vasco Gomez was busily at work upon his almost completed boat, that he first felt himself definitely alone.

To him it was a strange sensation. So strange, in fact, that when he received the first impact of it, the knife which he was using dropped from his hand as if something had struck him on the wrist. Then, after a moment, he picked up the knife again. But the feeling persisted.

His life, to say the least of it, had been an active and a crowded one. He had dealt with men and women and they had dealt with him, but never without physical impact. If he were to gaze back through the last score of years, he would hardly be able to find a single waking moment, even in shipwreck, when he had been entirely alone, divided from the world. He was alone now.

He was alone, and with that knowledge came thought. He was not used to thinking—Vasco Gomez—least of all to thinking about himself.

The work he was doing took up some of his thought but not all of it—not enough. Before, in the pauses of action, there had always been the treasure to think about, to plan for. Now the treasure was here. That space in his mind was suddenly filled by other, unaccustomed thoughts.

"Who is this fellow, Vasco Gomez?" he found himself thinking after a while, beset with a queer fear.

"Vasco Gomez? Why, that's you—that's me—you're here, man—you're making a boat!" He said the words aloud; they comforted him. But after a while he began to think again.

Vasco Gomez—he certainly knew who Vasco Gomez was! He saw him fighting, drinking, kissing a wench's shoulder, climbing a ship's red side with a long knife bitten in his teeth. A big, scarred bull of a man, solid and awe-inspiring.

But that wasn't Vasco Gomez any more. Vasco Gomez was here. Vasco Gomez was here—and entirely alone.

He felt himself diminish as he thought the words—

diminish as the brig had diminished. The brig, too, had been solid and bulky at first—then smaller—then a puppet —a speck on the sea. So now with him. He saw a little man on a toy island—an ant-size figure set down on a spoonful of land in the midst of blue immensities.

His face dripped with sweat, though he had not been working hard. The rasp of his knife on the wood made an acute and lonely sound. It seemed to him that he could hear that small sound go out and out, through infinities of water and air, and still meet no other sound that could be its fellow—and still—meet—no—other—sound.

His mind righted itself with a jerk. No, he had the clue to his thinking. He had been on the island for very nearly five months, as he reckoned. Well, he knew what happened sometimes to men so marooned, the look they got in their eyes, the voices they thought they heard.

He had not expected this to happen to him; he was too strong, too clever. But if it were so, so be it—he now knew where the danger lay and could guard against it. As soon as he had settled this in his mind, he felt restored. The sky and sea shrank back to their proper proportions.

He had hardly expected to finish the boat in less than ten days, but a fury of work took hold of him. While he toiled, he could not diminish—the sky and sea held their places. He found himself now and then trying over sentences in the jargon the Indians spoke. He caught himself listening thirstily as the sentences fell from his mouth. Only they lacked something—they lacked the note of a voice that was not his own.

In four days the boat was finished and afloat in the cove.

He had been gathering provisions during the last months. He had even made a keg for his water. It took no time at all to put these aboard or to rig his improvised sail. He wondered at himself, while he laboured, that he laboured so feverishly. Surely it did not matter if he set sail in a week or a month, now the season of storms was past. But, in these last days, time was no longer the one long hour that belonged to him and his treasure. It had become again a sifting of hasty grains through the blue hour-glass of the sky—and each grain that fell seemed to steal a little strength from his heart.

He stood up at last, hot and sweating. Night had fallen. All was ready now, except for the actual lifting of the treasure—and it was not sensible to begin that work at night. But he woke before the dawn.

When he had wakened, he lay there a moment without moving; entirely happy. He had known many women in his life, but to-day was the day of his true nuptials.

The sun was sinking when he uncovered the final chest. He struck a great blow with his axe at a rusty lock and stared. It was the bridal. The gold seemed to leap up at him.

Next moment he was down among it, both fists were full. He felt as if he had been running, his breath came and went in the runner's gasp. How good it was to touch, how thick and heavy and smooth—better than any woman's shoulder —better than bread!

Slowly, luxuriously, he broke open the other chests. It was all there—idol and pyx—blood-ruby and rough-cut emerald—the grandee's studded scabbard—the soft masks of virgin gold that the heathen priests had worn. He had dreamed of it as a king's ransom—he smiled at the poverty of his dreams.

The abrupt night came, shut down, but he did not stir. He did not light a fire, he did not go back to his hut. Time had resumed its long hour—time was not. He lay all night in the pit, he was perfectly happy.

The dawn came and he rose, but not as he had risen twenty-four hours ago. That morning, when he got up, he was still poor and an adventurer; this morning he got up rich, with the cares of riches.

He laughed when he thought of his furious labour of the last few days. Time was his friend, not his enemy, there was no need to fight it. The boat was ready—put the gold aboard—cast off—and everything else would follow, as the ship's wake follows the ship.

The business of the Indians first. They were his friends, but even so they would not do all he wanted without reward. Well, there he could get off cheaply—they hardly knew the uses of the yellow metal. But then there was the Governor's friend and the Governor himself—and he frowned. Everything could be bought with a price, no doubt, but, even for the rich, certain things came high.

He knew, none better, what palms would have to be greased.

If it had but matched with the poverty of his dreams—even then, he saw the difficulty. But this king's ransom—why even the king himself might want a finger in the pie!

Yesterday, he would gladly have given half the treasure to get off safe with the other half. But now he had seen it and touched it.

A dull anger began to rise in him. What business had all these strangers, meddling with his treasure? They hadn't schemed for it or found it.

Now he saw them, one and all, roosted around the edge of the pit like vultures—the Indians, the Governors, the lawyers and courtiers, the women with thirsty eyes, a bishop even, a red-hatted cardinal. Yes, even the Church itself, even God Himself exacted a portion of the treasure! They came closer, they stretched out their hands, bit by bit, drop by drop, then bled him of his precious gold. They gave him empty, useless things in return—a kiss—a patent of nobility—an altar of rose-marble—but the bleeding never ceased. At last, an old man, he crouched over the pitiful remnant of a king's ransom—and even then there were creatures coming to bleed him anew. He waved his arm in the air to drive off the vision.

Decidedly, he would have to revise his plans. He hurriedly tried to think of the least—the very least—he must spend to be safe. He pared his bribes down and down—and yet the total appalled him.

Then the mere passage of time brought with it a certain balm. After all, he did not have to set sail till he wished. He would eat and drink and sleep and play with his treasure—and in time some perfect plan might come to him.

The hours slipped into days, the days into weeks. One evening, notching his calendar-stick, he realised with a start that it was nearly two months since he had first uncovered the treasure. It seemed impossible, but it was true.

Well, Vasco Gomez, he thought with an odd lethargy, it is time you were setting off, my friend—to-morrow we will begin.

The morrow came, the sea seemed calm as a mill pond. And yet, far down to the south—was not that the edge of a cloud? He shook himself impatiently—was he losing his mind?—a sailor and afraid of a speck of white? With dragging steps, he turned toward his boat. Then a rescuing thought came to him—the bags for the treasure. The old bags were rotten—he would have to devise new bags, new chests. He felt at peace again immediately; he spent the morning happily, selecting the wood for his chests.

They were finished at last, but not before the stormy season. Vasco Gomez was no madman—he would not put out with such a cargo till the storms were done.

Meanwhile, with his treasure about him, Vasco Gomez lived many lives. Up till now, his life had left him little time for imagination beyond the needs of the day, but now his imagination flowered like a great poppy—his dreams spread a scarlet cloth for his bare feet to tread.

At first they were the simple visions and Elysiums of any sailor—enough food and drink, the easy girls of the ports— but as time went on they grew more elaborate, more refined, more clearly intense. He feasted delicately; music played while he feasted; the wines, poured for him, were the rarest of their kind. He did not gorge or lie drunken. When he went to take the air, outriders went before him; the king called him cousin and kissed him on the cheek. And when he returned to his palace, it was no girl of the ports whose lips were turned to him, but a king's daughter, a mermaid, a creature of light and foam. Sometimes she was dark as the soft nights, sometimes golden as the first spear of morning. It did not matter—she was whatever he wished, she was all women he had known, yet she was always new.

Then his power broadened, his shadow increased. He made wars and calmed them, raised one nation and put down another, appeased famine, tamed the seas. The king no longer called him cousin—he threw the king bones from his table and the king was grateful. Men whispered among themselves that only the protected of heaven could cast such a shade. And, indeed, to this man came messengers not wholly of this world.

Gomez, walking one morning when the season of storms had passed, came suddenly upon a boat, beached high and dry, protected by a rude shelter. For a moment he stared at it without recognition. Then he remembered—it was his boat, and he would never find better weather for his journey.

He looked the boat over carefully. The storms had not touched her—she was seaworthy still. He launched her in the cove again. Then he went slowly to the place where his chests were kept, and loaded them aboard. Only one thing remained, to fill the chests with the treasure. He dropped a rose-noble in one chest—it made a queer sound on the wood. Then he started for the rest of the treasure.

Two hours later, he sat in the boat, with his head in his hands. He had built his boat too small for the weight she was to carry.

Well, he must build another boat, that was all. But, as he thought this, he knew that even if he could build a boat big enough to bear that weight of gold, the boat would take more than one man to handle.

He could ferry what he now had aboard to the other island, bury it, come back for more. That meant a thousand risks with every voyage. He had lived with his treasure too long. He could not bear to bury a part of it elsewhere and leave it.

Well then, he would put it back in Pedro's old cache, taking only enough away with him to make a fresh start. Hire a ship—come back—to let other men into his secret— to go shares from the very first in what was his alone.

He thought for a long time, wearily revolving plans in his head. He knew that he could follow none of them. There must be another plan. All things were to be bought, if one had gold enough.

He lay all night in the boat, thinking. Morning came at length, and his riddle was still unsolved, but for a while he had ceased to think of it.

He had gone back, for a moment, to one of his many dreams. It was quite a simple dream and made but a poor show among his more ornate visions, yet he liked to dream it, at times.

He saw a tumbledown wine-shop with a dried bush over the door, on the crest of a hill road in Portugal. There was a girl in the wine-shop, a girl with fresh lips and hair as black as her comb.

She had a soldier for a lover, and a proud heart. Gomez was poor and a thief—it was in the days before he went to sea. They drove him away from the wine-shop often enough, but he came back to it. Once the soldier beat him, he took the beating with shut lips. The girl looked on, smiling. When at last Gomez saw that it was useless, he left the soldier in a mountain gully with a knife in his back and ran away before they caught him. Then his real life began.

In Gomez's dream, however, there was no soldier. There was only the girl, and himself as he had been at that time. But she was no longer scornful and they smiled at each other between the kisses.

The dream seemed very real to him, this time. He leaned over the side of the boat and stared at the water idly.

There was a face, reflected in the water. He observed it as he might the face of a stranger at first.

His own face was the face of the boy in his dream—a young, sharp face, ready for good or evil, but as yet not deeply marked with either—the face of youth. This was the withered face of an old man.

Slowly and wonderingly, he passed his hands over his body, regarded his legs, his arms. He had not looked at himself for a long time. But this scarecrow was he. "You've come a long way, Gomez," he muttered.

A new picture came to him, out of his other dreams. The splendid Vasco Gomez, the lord of the treasure, in his fine bed alone. The breath came faintly from the lips of the dying man. On one side of the bed was seated a priest, on the other a lawyer, but the dying eyes saw neither crucifix nor testament. They were staring ahead into darkness, trying to see something they could not fix upon. Outside the door, a servant kept back a silent throng—the throng of the claimants, the inheritors. A black-gloved personage waited in a corner, without impatience. Every man's end.

If some miracle—some incredible bribing of God—could set him ashore on the mainland, with his treasure! Even so, there were only so many lives in the world to live. And, already, he had lived those lives. If not in the body, yet very completely, very thoroughly. The body could do no more for him, the treasure could do no more. All but the one picture of the girl and the wine-shop—and that no treasure could repurchase, for it belonged to a past year.

Vasco Gomez braced one hand in the other hand till the muscles in his back stood out. He had always been a strong man, a clever and wary fighter. Now he must fight again, without ruth or scruple or weakness, as in the old days. But this time the adversary was invisible.

The next morning found him walking the beach, still fighting. Now and then he looked out to sea. It was very calm and clear. Then he realised that even the sea was a servant of his adversary, and turned his eyes away.

He sat down in the sand at last, arms lax, heart and body worn out. He was very tired but he would not give up the fight while breath was in him.

Everything to be bought with gold, he repeated to himself doggedly. One cannot fail with money—everything with a price in money—men—governors—kings—old age—God Himself, at the last. . . .

The wave came from afar—he could hear it coming. He braced himself to meet it, but it was too late. It was no wave of the sea, the sea was quiet enough. This wave gathered—rose—burst over him. He felt the shock, and trembled. He was beaten now.

Everything to be bought with gold, up to God Himself. Not without exception. You could buy much. You could buy candles and masses. But God, at the last, was not to be bought. That was the truth.

Slowly, without revulsion or outcry, for he was beaten, he lay on the sand and felt the cells of his body drink in this truth. After a long while a little stirring of peace began to move in his breast.

He rose at last. He felt weak when he had risen, and when he moved, his steps were the steps of an old man. But he would have strength enough for the work that remained.

He went back to the little cove where his boat was moored, and stood for a moment gazing at the water. Yes, that was the place. He had swum there often but never yet found bottom. The bottom must be very deep.

He took the piece of his treasure nearest to hand—it was one of the golden masks—and let it fall from his hand into the water. It shimmered as it went down, then that too was lost. He gave a sharp sigh, stooped stiffly and picked up the grandee's sword.

At last only the rose-noble was left. He weighed it in his hand a moment, as curiously as if it had been a sea-shell. It had a man's face on one side—the man had a nose like Pedro's. Strange, to put a man's face on a thing like that! He let it fall—it shone through green glooms and was gone.

Up till now, each piece that he had let fall had seemed to carry a small portion of his soul with it as it sank. But now, when there was no more treasure to drown, he felt otherwise. His soul could be divided no longer. It was either here in his body or down under the water with the treasure —but it did not matter, for, wherever it was, it was not in morsels.

He stared at the water anew with mild curiosity. A fish was swimming where the rose-noble had shimmered.

After a while, he wandered back to the beach and sat looking out toward the sea. For a moment he thought of his lost battle, but not with pain or shame. He had fought well and long. Now the fight was over. He would not fight again. There had been only one battle after all—it had lasted all his life—but he was done with it now.

He could not have eaten food for a long time. A day, perhaps more than a day? He could not remember. But when he thought of food, the thought revolted him. He was hungry now, but he was not hungry for bread.

The night fell and found him still on the beach. He thought of going back to his hut, but did not do so. Instead, he moved farther up the beach and ensconced himself in a sort of niche—where one boulder overhung another. The bottom boulder was raised—it was out of the way of the landcrabs—the top one was almost a roof. He sat there, with his back propped by the rear of the niche, his hands on his knees. The night air was cool and pleasant, the stars had come out. He looked out over the sea and felt the cool air on his face. There was a horizon there, hidden away in that gulf of starry darkness, but he was not seeking that horizon.

After some hours, he moved a little and spoke. "You've come a long way, Vasco Gomez," he said anew, with a certain touch of affirmation. Nothing replied to the words.

Some eight months later, H.M.S. *Vixen*, sloop-of-war, blown out of her course by contrary gales, sent a boat ashore to the island in the hope of finding fresh water and fruit for a crew already in danger of scurvy. The lieutenant in charge of the landing-party proceeded with all due precaution at first. But when the water-casks had been filled, and it was evident that the island was uninhabited, he allowed his men some liberty, and himself strolled down the beach.

It was a pretty beach, and seemed to encircle the island completely. He had got this far in his musings when a shout from one of the men farther down the beach made him clap his hands to his cutlass. Then he saw that the man was standing up and waving his arms. He walked hurriedly.

The buzzing group of sailors fell back before him. He found himself abruptly face to face with a stranger. The man was seated in a species of natural niche made by two boulders, his hands on his knees in an attitude of contemplation, his eyes staring out to sea. Some rags of clothing still clung to him and the crabs had not even touched him, but his whole body was the colour and texture of leather. He must have been dead for a number of months—what remained was a mummy that the sun and the wind had embalmed between them. Yet the features were quite recognisable—there was even an expression upon them—an expression that the lieutenant had seen before. He touched his lips with his handkerchief, remembering the last time he had seen it. No, even the sun and the wind could not account entirely for that emancipation.

A sailor was at his elbow, pulling a forelock.

"Do you know who that is, sir?" he said, in an eager voice. "It's Gomez, the bloody pirate, sir—I seen him before and so has Tom—and serve him right, the Portugee devil, that's what I say!"

"Yes," said the lieutenant, hardly listening, "it may well be he. We heard he had been marooned and——"

"Marooned is right, sir," said the sailor, "the bloody villain! Even his own crew got sick of him at the last and ——" He leaned forward as if to spit upon the leathered image.

"Keep your wits about you, my man!" said the lieutenant, sternly, and the sailor retired. Now he and his fellows were reciting the dead man's crimes, but the lieutenant did not hear them.

He was looking at Vasco Gomez. He must be right—you could not mistake that expression, once you had seen it. And yet he could not understand.

His eyes travelled down the beach to the land crabs scuttling busily—yes, there were turtles, beyond there— fruit inland, fish in the sea. A small island, but provision enough to feed a whole ship's crew.

"And yet I could swear that the man died of hunger," muttered the lieutenant to himself. "It is strange."

THEY HAD BEEN TOGETHER a great many times, on a great many beaches, in a great many restaurants, looking out over the water. The restaurants had been called by various names in various languages—they had had orchestras and dance-bands and juke-boxes and a little man who played a guitar and a girl who played an accordeon. They had been full of sailors in berets and Futurist painters, also in berets, and women in evening dress and women with monocles and women in slacks and men in tail-coats and women also in tail-coats and men with their bare feet stuck in espadrilles. This one was called Mrs. Sims' Clam House and, except for two tanned children solemnly eating strawberry ice-cream at the counter, it was entirely empty when they came in.

They moved to the small corner table overlooking the water and sat down. The table was supposed to seat four but they pulled up the clean, hard chairs and made it do for seven. They never minded things like that—they had done them many times. They were not particularly demanding—they merely wanted the best, and the new place was always the best. After a while, it got spoiled and they left and found another place. They left while the crowds were still coming and before the receivers came. But only the local people and a few summer colonists yet came to Mrs. Sims' Clam House. It was as new a place as that.

"It's frantic," said Jinny Crick, taking off her sunglasses and slipping them into the special compartment in the special handbag, "look at the boats. It's heavenly. Isn't it frantic?"

"It's a nice little place," said Beth Blake, in her rich voice. " We think it's a nice little place." She looked at the waitress. "Good-evening, Pearl," she said pleasantly. "Fish-chowder, crab-buns and the salad for all of us." She smiled. "I won't let them have anything else," she said, "even if they cry and scream for it. They mustn't have another thing."

"Well, that's all right, I guess, Mrs. Blake," said the waitress in a small, indomitable voice. "Tea, coffee or milk?"

"Black coffee, very hot, in very thick china cups," said the small man unexpectedly and deeply. His name was Harry Crandall and, though he had flown from the Coast two days before, the noise of the airplane was not quite out of his head. "But they must be thick china—diner china," he added anxiously, peering at the waitress.

"I guess we got them thick enough if that's what you want," said the waitress.

"Splendid!" said Harry Crandall. "And that is just what I want." He looked around the small, new place. "Thank God there aren't any curtains," he said. "I was afraid of red-checked ones. And matches that look like little sailors. But it isn't. No offence meant to the Navy," he added to the blond young man in ensign's uniform on the other side of Jinny Crick, "but I just don't happen to like matches that look like little sailors."

"You want some matches?" said the waitress.

"No thank you," said Harry Crandall, abstractedly, "I want no matches. I match no want-ads. I just keep rolling along." He smiled, secretly. The waitress looked at him doubtfully for a moment and then disappeared toward the kitchen.

"How was the Coast?" said Jinny Crick. "Did you see Jimmy and Mike?"

"No," said Harry Crandall, "Jimmy's in the Signal Corps. And Mike was out at Palm Springs, rewriting the story-line for 'Little Dorrit.' It's going to be Colossal's new contribution to Anglo-American friendship. They've changed it a little, of course. Little Dorrit is a waif brought up in the Romney Marshes and she takes a fishing-trawler over to Dunkerque—if you believe Mike, over the telephone. As a matter of fact, it will probably turn out to be a good picture, Mike has a knack."

"A knack and a promise," said Beth Blake. "A knack in his engine. How's the newest bride?"

"She's the best society of Cedarhurst," said Harry Crandall. "But I like Mike. I always did."

"We all love Mike," said Jinny Crick. "It's just the brides

and the clothes that get us down. The last time I saw him he had on a shirt with pores in it. But I suppose that's the Coast."

The ensign, who had been trying to follow these remarks, turning his head politely toward each speaker in turn, now addressed Harry Crandall.

"Were you out there making a picture yourself, sir?" he said, respectfully.

"No," said Harry Crandall. "This was a radio-show. Propaganda." He bit off the word.

"It must have been very good stuff, sir," said the ensign, again respectfully and attacked his chowder. The red-haired girl sitting opposite him tried to smile at him but could not catch his eye. Poor Tom—it was all her fault and she had let him in for it. But his train went at 9.38 and there wouldn't be much longer now.

All the same, she was glad that he had seen them, and seen them as they were. It would make things so much easier to explain, later on. Though older people were always hard to explain.

She sat in a little pool of silence, quite contented to be opposite Tom, while around her the swift talk flowed—the casual conversation, full of names and jokes, jumping gaps to the next new thing—the patter and the lingo. She had been brought up on it, she had been brought up on them all. It went back to French sands and the rocking sleep on trains and liners and all the wonderful people, coming in through the garden for cocktails, sitting out on the terrace and talking, coming up the stairs to the studio and making a pleasant noise. Aunt Beth and Uncle Charlie and the nice man they all called Monkey and all the others. At one time, many years ago—nearly five years ago when she was only fifteen—she had thought them the most wonderful people in the world. Then Mummy and Daddy had finally broken up and, since then, she had been away a great deal at schools and camps and colleges. So, since then, she hadn't really seen very much of them, though she had dutifully read their books and seen their plays and their paintings and their pictures in magazines—even boasted of them, now and then, at new schools, when you had to boast of something. And they had remembered birthdays and graduations and vacations—remembered them with thoughtful and difficult presents and telegrams from California and offers of trips and week-ends that she'd stopped accepting once she began to build her life for herself. And all of that had been genuine, and she granted it. But it wasn't her kind of life any more at all.

She glanced around the table, seeing them with the hard, clear eyes of youth. It was hard to grow up and see them as they were, and yet it had to be done. Aunt Beth and Uncle Charlie—Sid Vining, the stage-designer—Harry Crandall, the writer—Jinny Crick who was always there because she was always there. They looked harmless enough and she had been fond of them all. But they were the generation that had made the trouble—and you couldn't forget about that. They had gotten the world in a mess, and it was her generation and Tom's that would have to straighten it out. They had gotten the world in a mess, they and wonderful people like them. They had shouted for peace and disarmament—they had shouted of the horrors of war—then they had turned around and shouted for war. They drank too much, they divorced too easily, they lived by a code of their own, there was no health in them. So, they ought to behave as if there were no health in them. And yet, even now, they didn't behave that way—and that was the irritating fact. They were eating, instead, with the serious and absorbed attention they always gave to good food.

"Don't tell me that's saffron," said Sid Vining, "because I wouldn't believe you. But it is."

"They get it from a little shop in Weymouth. All the way from Weymouth," said Beth Blake.

"It could be a mint, you know," said Sid Vining, earnestly, "with the food as good as this. Remember the place at St. Tropez?"

"They didn't ration gas at St. Tropez," said Jinny Crick. "That's a song-title, isn't it, Ensign?"

"I guess it really is," said Tom Finlay, smiling pleasantly. The red-haired girl felt a sudden desire to touch him, to reassure herself of his solid reality. For Sid Vining was talking now of the things that could be done with Mrs.

Sims' Clam House, and, as the others threw in their quick, light comments, the little place changed and grew. Quietly but inexorably it grew and the large cars slid up to the dock and the chattering people flooded in—the tanned men in white dinner-jackets, the pleasantly-scented women who threw their little fur wraps over the backs of the hard, bare chairs and sat on stools at the bar and thought it was quaint and darling. It grew, as places always grew, when the wonderful people came and until they left.

She wanted to pound on the table and say, "Stop it! Stop it!" But Harry Crandall caught her eye and smiled.

"What's the matter?" he said. "It isn't going to happen, you know. It couldn't any more."

"You wouldn't understand," she said. "The boats out there are real boats and they catch real fish. It isn't just a— a stage-set for——"

"For people like us?" he said. "No, the point is well taken. It isn't a stage-set any more."

"I guess I'm being rude," said the girl. "I guess maybe I am. But what was the Hotel du Cap like, at Antibes, the last time you saw it?"

"They were quartering Senegalese there," said Harry Crandall and shrugged. "Well, they had to—I wish they'd quartered more. But it was nice, out on the rocks—you must remember."

"I remember all right," said the girl. "I remember those fine old days and the screaming parties and the Russian woman who jumped out of the window. I wasn't particularly old but I remember."

"You're lucky," said Harry Crandall. "Even with that. I didn't get over till I was in the Army."

"If you want the child's point of view—well, it wasn't much fun," said the girl. "We all wanted ice-cream sodas and American clothes and movies that weren't months late. We wanted the funnies and games like the ones we read about, and not to be foreign."

"That's interesting," said Harry Crandall. "Yes, I see how that could be."

The girl stared at him. That was another thing about them that she had forgotten—they were always so open-

125

E

minded. They'd attack you for a taste, demolish you for a judgment—but not for an opinion, particularly when it was critical of them.

"I suppose that's why I used to be an isolationist," she said. "It hurt Mummy and Daddy. They couldn't understand it."

"Perfectly natural reaction." said Harry Crandall.

"But how can you say that?" said the girl. "Ever since the war first broke out, you——"

He looked at her and his face was empty and sad.

"After the last war," he said, "the one thing I swore I'd never write was propaganda. But this one is for our skins, and the chips are down." He smiled at her. "So no explanations or apologies," he said. "Have some coffee. It's good "

She tried to read the pleasant, lined, empty face. There could be nothing there of importance to her—she knew that when she looked at Tom. And yet, the eyes were alive as a prodigal child's. But the prodigal children were finished.

"And, speaking of blackouts, Beth," said Charles Blake, "as we weren't."

"Yes, we should," said Beth Blake and again, like migratory birds, they collected themselves and began to make gestures of departure. It took a little time but it was efficient and smooth. They said good-bye, carefully and politely, to Pearl, to Mrs. Sims, to the man at the counter. They looked into the kitchen for a moment, they walked out on the dock and looked at the sunset. It was obvious to the red-haired girl that they should lower their voices on the dock and be less themselves than they were, but they did nothing of the sort. It was obvious that the other people on the dock should hate them, but that did not seem to happen either.

When, at last, she and Tom were in the small car together, the girl gave a sigh of relief.

"Let's drive back by the Point, Tom," she said. "It's only half a mile further and we needn't be back right away."

"Well, they're very interesting people," said Tom, a little later, "they certainly give you something to think about." He laughed, a little nervously. "Was I all right, darling?" he said.

"You were fine," said the girl, "just fine. And you don't have to be polite."

"Well, they were polite to me," said Tom, and she saw the stubborn line of his jaw.

"They always are, while you're with them," said the girl. "Oh, don't let's quarrel," she said.

"I wasn't quarrelling, beautiful," said Tom and they both stared out over the darkening water. He was there and solid and the way she wanted him to be. And they should be talking a great deal and they were not talking at all. The wonderful people had spoiled it.

"Oh, damn them!" she said with sudden violence. "Damn them from hell to breakfast! Damn them all!"

"Why, honey," he said. "Why, honey—what's the matter?" Then his arms were around her and she should have felt safe and secure. But there was neither safety nor security anywhere, any more. The wonderful people had seen to that, long ago, when they first set a match to the world.

"Oh—it's all right," she said. "It's all right, Tom. But we've got to get to your train."

When she returned to the house, the blackout shades were already drawn and the highball tray was waiting. Beth Blake was explaining about the blackout shades.

"It's just dim-out, really," she was saying. "But we thought we'd do it rather thoroughly, since we had to." She gestured at the gay, bright flower-patterns on the inside of the shades, "Jimmy Bender thought they ought to be much more Dali," she said. "He said he'd do them over, but I don't think Dali's very cosy for a blackout. I'd hate to look at eyes and watches while I was being bombed. So we just made them pretty-pretty and now Charlie says it's like living inside a seed-catalogue." Her rich laugh rang. She turned to the red-haired girl. "I hope your young man got a seat on the train," she said. "They're so tiresomely crowded, now, especially on week-ends."

"Oh, he got one all right," said the red-haired girl. "No thanks, Uncle Charlie, not a drink right now—I just want to powder my nose."

And there goes a very nice youngster who's just seen a ghost, thought Harry Crandall, watching her stride from the room. *But the young are so hard to reach. Were we as hard to reach as that? Well, yes, I suppose we were.*

He removed himself unobtrusively from the group and sat quietly in a corner, listening to the phonograph, his highball balanced on one knee. Charlie Blake was playing a new calypso—he always found them somehow.

"Telling you about the battle of Midway when those Japanese ships went down," went the strange, effective voice. "Telling you about the battle of Midway when the U.S. Navy fleet went to town——"

Harry Crandall listened, glad for the fact of noise. He'd talk, if he had to, in a minute, but right now he didn't want to talk, even to Charlie or Beth. And Charlie and Beth wouldn't mind—they had been together long enough.

He tried to remember when he had first met the Blakes— 21? 22? But it was hard to remember when you were tired. He'd met them with Steve Searle, who was dead of a heart attack, and Mimi Post, who wouldn't get out of her sanatorium now, and a lot of the old crowd. But it had been a new crowd, then—quite new and shiny. In the days of the Dome and the Rotonda and Marta's down in the Village and the start of many things—the days of the fierce bursts of work and the quick trips on liners—the days when Paris was Mecca and there wouldn't be any more wars. Yes, a new crowd—quite new and shiny. And everybody had been poor, at the start, except the Blakes. But nobody minded the Blakes not being poor.

Well, he thought, we've had a good run for it, money or no money. We've had what won't be again—the food and the talk and the wine. But France fell, dammit—France fell. She couldn't fall but she did. And that handsome youngster probably thinks it happened because they liked good food and things in proportion. But that's part of what you want to preserve. Not all, but part.

He looked around the room at the good faces—the faces of his friends. They had been together so often and so long and through so many happenings. The work was a different thing, that, in time could be assessed. Not such bad work either, on the whole, though no doubt it could have been better. But he was thinking of the people, not the work. For nobody was going to be able to put in a book what Charlie Blake was like twenty years ago or why Jinny Crick, for all her mannered folly, had both charm and heart. It couldn't be put in a book or explained to the young. But these are my friends, my colleagues, my generation—the people I have chosen to live and die beside. And we went on a queer adventure, very queer when you come to think of it—for it brought us back precisely, and in twenty years, to the things we had left behind, and now we must fight for those, if anything good is to live. And after that, we'll be old. But we've seen some things.

He noticed that the red-haired girl was back in the room again, on a sofa beside Sid Vining. *Well, here goes for a rescue,* he thought. *She won't get on with Sid—not in whatever mood she's in—and Sid's pretty on edge himself. And I don't want Beth's party ruined—even if it's a small one.*

He approached them amiably. "Nice drinks? Nice picture-postcards, gentleman and lady?" he said. "Nice guide for the conducted tour?"

"Don't give her a drink," said Sid Vining, sourly. "She thinks it's the Demon Rum." He rose and bowed "I have been rebuked by infants," he said. "I shall now go and get myself stinking in comparative peace." He stalked away.

"Well," said Harry Crandall and sat down. The girl said nothing. "He won't, you know," said Harry Crandall, "in case you wanted information."

"Who cares if he does?" said the girl, in a low, fierce voice. Harry Crandall considered this.

"Oh—some of us—in a way," he said. "It isn't particularly good for his work. And he's about the best scene designer we've got. But he's been mostly on the wagon for quite a while, now."

"Then why doesn't he *do* something?" said the girl. "Instead of talking about putting little bars in restaurants. Why doesn't he do camouflage?"

He stared at her and laughed.

"Poor Sid," he said. "He's got a trick knee. And bad eyes. The Army's turned him down twice. Now he thinks they may take him but he isn't sure. So he's a little touchy."

129

"Oh," said the girl.

"Yes," said Harry Crandall. "And now I'd really better get you a drink. You've had a white face all evening and I don't like girls with white faces. Also, I need one myself. You get tired, on planes—it's the monotony, I guess."

He mixed two drinks, expertly, thinking, *Harry Crandall, the rescuer, Harry Crandall, the life guard! Aren't you proud of yourself, Mr. Harry Fix-it Crandall? But Howdy and Ella Martinson were friends of yours and swell people, so the least you can do is to get their daughter a drink at a party. That will help so much.*

When he brought them back, the girl looked at hers doubtfully.

"I don't really like it," she said.

"I am not attempting to inebriate you," said Harry Crandall, patiently. "I am recommending for shock. And don't tell me you haven't had one."

"I haven't," said the girl, but she sipped at the very light highball.

"Of course not," said Harry Crandall. "Your generation doesn't. You live on milk and pepsi-cola and grow to be six-feet three. Which is perfectly fine and I'm for it. But nobody's shockproof, these days. Nobody at all."

"It wasn't anything at all," said the girl, but the colour began to come back to her white face.

"Of course it wasn't anything." said Harry Crandall.

"It was just driving back through the blackout," said the girl, "I mean, it takes quite a long time. I—I didn't realize it would take so long. It was *spooky!*" she said, with hurt.

"That so?" said Harry Crandall. "Yes, that must make tough driving." He did not say, "In the last war, I remember the first time we moved with lights, after the Armistice. I remember that because it hit you right in the face—it scared you for a minute. And I remember how London looked, at the start of this one." He did not say any of those things.

"And then I came back——" said the girl. "And I'd just seen Tom off—and Aunt Beth was talking about black-out shades and being silly—and I went upstairs to powder my nose in her bedroom—and she's got a very bright tin pail full of very white sand—and I guess it matches the bedroom—and oh!——"

"Nobody will notice it, if your cry," said Harry Crandall. "Or we could go out in the kitchen. People often do."

"I'm not going to cry!" said the girl. "But it suddenly got rather horrible. And Aunt Jinny—Mrs. Crick—was in the bedroom. She was sitting there in a chair and she was crying. But she wasn't making any sound—just the tears coming out of her eyes. And I stood there like a fool and didn't know what to do!" Her voice rose sharply.

"That's quite all right," said Harry Crandall, carefully. "You see, Jinny has a boy in the Coastal Patrol. You played with him once but you probably wouldn't remember him— his name's Sam Langley and he's even taller than you are. Red hair, too," he said reflectively. "Well, you see how that might worry her. And then Toby Crick's in London for Lease-Lend, and she's rather fond of Toby."

"If you're trying to make me feel like even more of a heel, you're succeeding very nicely." said the girl.

"Oh, no," said Harry Crandall. "No, I'm not claiming the higher maternal virtues for Jinny—in fact, I'd hate to be mothered by her, myself. But I'd hate not to have her around, with her silly square make-up box, making up her silly face and worrying about it. You get to be that way about people, after a while, and its been a long while."

He sighed, for a moment. "So you fought with your young man," he said.

"I didn't fight with him," said the girl. "It was just—it was going to be wonderful—and then suddenly, it didn't mean anything."

"You can't go entirely by one week-end," said Harry Crandall, remarking that the girl's colour had now returned to normal. *And, Old Mother Hubbard, how did you pull that well-worn advice right out of the hat,* he thought.

"You don't understand," said the girl. "You couldn't, possibly! It's got to be right for me—after Mummy and Daddy and the way they broke up! It's got to be safe and secure! Something's got to be! And I thought Tom was and I was counting on that. I thought not even Aunt Beth and the rest of you could spoil him. And then——"

"And then," said Harry Crandall, "we exerted our well-known wiles?"

"Oh, it isn't what you did," said the girl. "You never do. But you made him look dull—and ordinary—and he was respectful to you—so horribly respectful——"

"In other words," said Harry Crandall, "he was polite." He cleared his throat. *I wish I could remember more about that young man,* he thought. *He was perfectly all right and I liked him but I never could pick him out in a parade.* "And as for his being dull," he said guardedly, "I thought he had some pretty solid ideas."

"Yes, that's Tom," said the girl, eagerly. She pulled her handkerchief from her handbag and firmly blew her nose. "And they're real ideas, too. He thinks there are going to be a lot of changes after the war and we'll all have to be more responsible."

"That's an interesting point of view," said Harry Crandall. *All the same, she'd better meet young Sam Langley,* he thought. *This Tom may be all she thinks but he ought to have more competition. And the first time you fall in love you're always so sure it's for keeps.* He cocked his ear to what the girl was saying now.

"But I can't get over being so scared," she said, like a child. "Why was I?"

"There's a war on," said Harry Crandall, "and a big one. And you can forget for a while, just the way you can almost go to sleep on a march. But, now and then, it comes over you, like a wave. It isn't a question of courage and it doesn't affect your doing things. You drove the car back all right—didn't you? You didn't drive it into a ditch? Well—that's all you have to know."

"Yes, that's so," she said gratefully. "I didn't drive it into the ditch."

"Remember that," said Harry Crandall, "because there was a big car and it got in the ditch. And now we've got to get it out. Not just your generation or mine," he said carefully, "but all of us. That's the difference. Do you hate us all very much? You might, you know. After all, we did have the parties."

"I don't know," said the girl. "I don't know."

"As for me, I'm entirely vulnerable," said Harry Crandall. "This is Charlie's last leave and Beth's going to shut the house. But I'm everything you think. I'm a nasty little civilian propagandist and will the new crowd make hay of that, in ten years' time, when it's all over? Remember the fearsome tripe the established names—or most of them—wrote about the last one and how it retched the bowels of my generation? Well, they'll retch at me, just the same way. But somebody had to do it." He spoke without heat or pride.

"I don't understand you," said the girl. "I don't understand any of you. I don't know that I want to."

"It doesn't matter a bit," said Harry Crandall. "Only maybe you'd better. If you're going to make a new world, and I gather you are." He looked at her, glad to see her so stiff and uncompromising. "Well, we were, too," he said. "And it wasn't a bad one. It had freedom and pleasure and good food and truthful art. But we had to make our own rules and we couldn't see around the next curve. So that's that, and what happened, happened." He stared at his drink. "And you'll do it very differently," he said.

"I should hope so," said the girl.

"That's all right," said Harry Crandall. "But remember that freedom means freedom, not bossing other people—and your friends, in the end, are your friends.

"With which profound remark," he said, "your cracker-barrel philosopher will now sign off." He finished his drink and stood up.

"Let's go outside for a minute," he said. "Charlie's got a perfectly devilish blackout arrangement on the terrace door, but I think I know my way through it."

When they were outside, in the cool darkness, the girl took a deep breath.

"It smells nice," she said. "It smells good. Even in wars."

"Yes," said Harry Crandall, gently. "You'll sleep, of course?" he said.

"Why, of course I'll sleep," said the girl. "Why shouldn't I?"

He chuckled faintly to himself. "No reason," he said. *But you're over your jitters,* he thought, *and you won't have the same kind again. You'll sleep like a baby and wake, and to-*

morrow you'll write to Tom, or he'll write to you. And you'll marry him or somebody, but it won't be me, thank goodness, for I've chosen the friends I must live and die beside. And we're getting on, every one of us, but we've got about one more kick in us and those that are left are tough. No, we won't be easy, in your Zion. But we'll try to behave. We're trying.

"Born and bred in the brier-patch, Brer Fox," he said, half to himself. "Born and bred in the brier-patch and now we're back there again. But we did take life with both hands —we weren't cautious about it. And that's still something to do."

But the girl was still standing there, breathing in the night, a tall, confident figure, beneath the calm sky that sometime might hold the planes. He smiled, nodded his head and went back to the house and his friends.

ACKNOWLEDGMENTS

Acknowledgments are due to Messrs. William Heinmann Ltd. for permission to reprint these stories.